Hattie Gee lived the first fifteen years of her life in the heart of the Yorkshire countryside. She had a carefree childhood, spending most of her time on a neighbouring farm. Her days were taken up with caring for the animals. This was where she developed a passion for nature. She found she had a special way with horses from a very young age.

When Hattie found her beautiful farm in Devon beside the sea, she believed this was her destiny. She had worked hard as a primary school teacher and brought up her three children. Now was her opportunity to combine her love of horses and children by starting up a riding school. It was a great success for many years and inspired her to write this story.

I would like to dedicate this book to my family. They are very patient with me and my busy life on the farm. My grandchildren give me hours of pleasure and I am so happy that they will all have this book I have written to read forever.

Hattie Gee

THE STOWAWAY

AUSTIN MACAULEY PUBLISHERS™

LONDON • CAMBRIDGE • NEW YORK • SHARJAH

A CIP catalogue record for this title is available from the British Library.

ISBN 9781398401211 (Paperback)
ISBN 9781398401228 (ePub e-book)

www.austinmacauley.com

First Published 2021
Austin Macauley Publishers Ltd®
1 Canada Square
Canary Wharf
London
E14 5AA

I would like to thank my writing group known as 'Jane's Girls' who have helped and encouraged me at every stage of the book. Also, my dearest friend Marilyn who has always read and enjoyed my work. Her enthusiasm gave me confidence to carry on. Thanks to Cornerstones for help with editing.

Synopsis

Hattie will never forget the day of the terrible storm, the shipwreck, the stowaway.

Finding Fado down a badger set behind the hen house on her farm changed her life. Hattie worked hard at her riding school. Caring for the horses was her passion but since her youngest daughter had left home, it was a hard and sometimes lonely life for her.

Fado was the eldest son of a servant family in Kenya. Since his father's death, his mother found life a struggle. When her new boss told her, she would not be able to work on his estate any more, she felt destitute. The only way to help her family, she thought, was to put her eldest son in a crate on the ship with the contents of her master's house. Tristan was returning to England to avoid his shady drug business from being discovered. After being found by Hattie, Fado thrived and grew strong. He became a good horseman who achieved his ambition to become a successful jockey.

Finally, Fado returned to Kenya to find and help his family.

Chapter 1

Hattie was having a rare moment to herself. The horses and ponies had been fed, watered, turned out in to their fields and there were no more riders booked in for today. Hattie sat down with a nice cup of tea and turned on the news.

"Just a minute!"

She stopped in the middle of a mouthful of cake.

"That's my beach. Wow, what a sight!"

NEWSFLASH was spread across the screen, interrupting the local story about solar panels in Cornwall.

"Breaking news shows a cargo ship has gone to ground and its entire contents are being washed up on an east Devon beach." the newsreader announced.

Hattie jumped off the sofa and grabbed her binoculars.

"Would you believe it? The size of those crates floating onto the beach; they look as big as that mobile home Geoff the farmhand has just given me!" exclaimed Hattie.

"Traffic jams are building up as people travel from surrounding coastal towns and villages to see the spectacle." continued the news reader.

Hattie observed her petite face with a perfect neckline that was adorned with a neat ring of pearls and matching earrings.

The woman has no idea about coping with the elements and the fury of the sea, thought Hattie. *I must get down there and see for myself.*

Hattie had never been the one to miss out on the action. She wasted no time in grabbing her coat and making her way down to the beach. Hattie could not have been prepared for the sight that met her eyes. People were wheeling Yamaha motorbikes over the pebbles and there were huge crates with all manner of things from nappies to tractor parts spilling out of them. There was a sea of people foraging for goods; a man over there was hauling a heavy piece of machinery while a lady at the other end of the beach was lifting as many bags of scientific dog food into her bag as she could carry.

Hattie wandered along head down carefully picking her way through the devastation. Was that a pot of her favourite face cream wrapped in seaweed? She bent down and un-wrapped the slimy brown strip to reveal the expensive cream she could rarely afford to treat herself to. Hattie put the pot back down as a guilty feeling overcame her. She stood over the lonesome pot and looked up. People all around her seemingly without a second thought were routing through the debris and taking the finest pickings.

"Why the heck shouldn't I take a small pot of cream when others are taking motorbikes?" Hattie muttered.

Hattie looked around to make sure that no one she knew was watching her and quickly snatched up the cream putting it into her bum bag. She walked away to another part of the beach where she was drawn to what looked like the contents of a house that had been stored in the big crate. A beautiful red and gold upholstered armchair, a huge walnut sideboard and a four-poster bed.

Well, this looks like some rich person's home contents, she thought. *I expect they will be able to afford replacements but some of these things look as if they would have had a sentimental value.*

Hattie was fascinated by an open chest with a large gold-rimmed hard-backed book on the top of it.

The book was titled, 'AFRICA' which intrigued Hattie and she sat down to read some of it. So engrossed was she that a familiar voice startled her.

"It was on the news; a rich businessman returning to England from South Africa has lost all of his worldly goods in the wreck."

Hattie had been on two horseback safaris in Africa and had loved everything about the country.

"Indeed, it is devastating, all their worldly goods washed up on the beach."

As she tried to get up, Hattie realised she had become quite stiff sitting on the cold and hard pebbles and had no idea how long she had been there. She turned onto her knees to haul herself up and as she did so, her head was poking inside the crate. She froze on all fours for a moment as she thought she heard a muffled sound. It was like a child's cry. She felt the hairs on the back of her neck stand up and could only let her imagination run away with her. She was jolted back to reality as she heard her neighbour call out.

"Here, give me your hand, I'll help you up."

Hattie walked off the beach clutching the book with her neighbour. They chatted on about the spectacle they had just been a part of. She looked back at the crate, thinking about the cry she had heard. Knowing what people thought of her when she mentioned her encounters with the spirits, she decided not to mention the noise to her neighbour.

When she arrived home, Hattie walked the dogs across her fields checking on all the horses and ponies and then went in to settle down for the evening with one of her favourite dinners; vegetarian moussaka, and the book about Africa.

Although life was a struggle sometimes, she had managed the place on her own after her second husband had decided it was not the life for him and fled. She missed her youngest daughter Ria terribly, since she had left home for university. Her eldest child Millie was going through a difficult time in London with infertility problems and was planning a move down near to her. Unfortunately, she was allergic to horses and would be of no help with the business. Her son Steve was definitely a Londoner and rarely came to visit the farm. His wife was either allergic or phobic to most things on it. Hattie was determined to make a go of the place as she believed it was her destiny to be there in the wonderful surroundings overlooking the sea.

Hattie had always been at one with nature. Her mother had described her as the wild one, only happy when out in the fields as a child. She had a passion for horses and her customers loved to ride them with her as she would tell stories about each of her horses and ponies as if she was that horse or pony herself. She trained them all with natural horsemanship and seemed to have complete harmony and telepathy with even the most troublesome ones.

Hattie's peace was short lived as a storm was brewing up, she had to wrap up in all her waterproofs and go around the farm making sure all the doors were bolted. She decided to bring the horses in as the rain started to lash down and she could hear the distant rumbling of thunder.

Whickering and jostling in nervous agitation at the gate, the horses seemed pleased to see her.

"Come on, you guys, I'll get you into your nice warm stables."

After putting their head collars on, she opened the gate and they obediently followed her up the track and into their stables. She knew the pony herd would not be as easy but the storm was getting closer and she thought they would be safer in their stables.

She battled her way past the hens shutting them up and onto the pony field.

"Come on, you lot, be good to me, into your stables."

Suddenly there was a loud crack of thunder. Hattie nearly lost her balance as all the ponies pushed through the gate and charged down the track. Two ran off behind the henhouse. She went after them; the dogs were there before her barking madly but not at the ponies. Bramble, the youngest lab, had her head down a hole while the other two were behind her. Hattie called them away as she knew there were fox holes and badgers around there, but she had to get the ponies away before the weather got any worse. She managed to chase the ponies out and caught up with the others waiting at the pony barn.

"In you go," she shouted at them as she opened the stable doors. "Phew!" she sighed, "what a relief all the horses and ponies are in and safe, but I am drenched!"

Hattie was making her way back to the house dreaming of a nice hot bath when she realised the dogs were not with her. She could hear them still barking behind the henhouse.

"Oh, come on, you dogs. I've had enough now," she shouted as she went towards them.

They wouldn't come to her; so, she got a long stick and beat the brambles and nettles down to get to them. They were barking at a badger set and when they saw her, they rushed over jumping up and licking her face before going back to the hole.

"Alright get down you lot, what is it?" Hattie followed them and peered down the hole.

She thought she could hear a noise but it was difficult due to the howling wind and rain and she put her head further down in the hole. There, peering up at her were two large brown and very frightened eyes.

"What the... who or what are you?" Hattie shouted down the hole.

She lay flat and reached her arm down inside the hole but there was no response. She got up, picked up the stick she had used earlier and put that down the hole, she felt a tug on it and pulled as hard as she could. To her horror, a small soaked mud splattered black child appeared at the top of the hole, hanging onto the stick. Hattie gathered him up in her arms and made her way back to the house with the dogs close at her heels.

"It's alright, love, you are safe now." She soothed the terrified dripping bundle.

When everyone was in the house, she shut the door and put the boy down but his legs buckled and he fell to the floor. She picked him up and grabbed the towel from the downstairs toilet.

"There you go; we'll soon have you warm and dry."

She wrapped him up in the towel trying not to look into his huge and frightened eyes. She peeled off her soaked waterproofs and boots.

"I'm afraid these have not done their job very well!" exclaimed Hattie as she shivered.

The poor boy was shivering and he was her priority. She picked him up and held him close to her whilst she carried him upstairs and ran the bath. She put some tea tree shower gel in and swished the water around with her free hand until soft white bubbles appeared. She thought the boy would love these as her own children had when they were young, but the boy clung tighter to her looking even more frightened.

"There's nothing to worry about, love, you'll soon feel nice and warm."

She lowered him into the bath and had to try and sponge him down with his arms still around her neck. The water was turning brown with the dirt coming off him. As she washed him, she sang to him to try and soothe him and he seemed to relax his grip. She managed to wash him all over and took a moment to have a look at him.

She thought he was between five and nine years old, he had a large tummy but she could also see his ribs and his little arms and legs were very thin. Tears came to her eyes as she lifted him out of the bath and wrapped him in a dry towel. She took him to the twin-bedded bedroom and lay him down on the single bed as she dried him. She kept her spare clothes in the wardrobe in this room.

Fishing around in the bags, she was relieved that she hadn't got round to taking the clothes to the charity shop.

Choosing a red fleece and a pair of pink leggings, she laughed and said to the boy,

"You won't win any fashion contest dressed like that!"

The boy seemed relieved to feel warm again; he was not to know what he looked like in the odd outfit. His eyes seemed to be closing and Hattie realised he must be exhausted.

"I don't think you're up to having some homemade soup." she told the boy as she put him in the bed.

He curled up, she stroked his little head and he was asleep within minutes. She crept out of the room and after having a hot shower, she put her pyjamas on and went downstairs to have some soup herself.

It wasn't until when she had finished her soup and when she had sat down at last relaxing with her feet up on the sofa that Hattie realised the enormity of what she had done. So far, she had dealt with the situation like she did with everything that was thrown at her in life. She went into automatic pilot and did what had to be done. But what should she do now? The poor child's huge frightened eyes kept flashing before her own. Of course, the next course of action should be to ring the police immediately. Hattie didn't want to frighten the poor little lad any more than he was with the police examining and questioning him.

Part of her found it very comforting to hold a little one in her arms again. It would be lovely to have a child to care for especially now that all her own children had left home, but she knew she wasn't doing the right thing by not reporting the boy.

Hattie got up and went to the phone. She picked up the yellow pages and looked up the number for social services. She knew there wouldn't be anyone there but thought it best to leave a message. This way at least the poor boy could get a decent night's sleep.

"Hello, my name is Hattie Gee from Sea Winds Farm. I want to report to you that I have found a boy on my farm today."

She left her mobile phone number for them to ring her back in the morning. It sounded slightly unbelievable, but at least she had done the right thing.

Hattie went back through the day; the shipwreck with the chest kept coming into her head, the book about Africa and the sound of crying coming out of the crate all came flooding back to her. Could this child be something to do with that crate full of contents from the house in Africa? Hattie fell asleep on the settee. She had vivid dreams of galloping across the Mara with the giraffe, zebra and wildebeest alongside her; then she was in the Maasai village, in a smoky mud hut surrounded by children and their goats. The next minute she was rocking up and down on a boat with the waves crashing over her head. Suddenly a wave tossed her out of the boat and she was sinking in the dark murky water, falling, falling deeper and deeper. She woke up with a jolt and ran upstairs to check on the boy but he was not in the bed!

Chapter 2

Fado

I was terrified when Mamma showed me the crate. She told me I was going to travel in it with the master's house contents to England. I had been helping his mamma to pack all the things in the big house for weeks. The master had gone to England already and left the Mara for good. There was a new master coming but he didn't want all the old masters' servants.

My father had been killed whilst protecting an American tourist from the jaws of a hippo. The group had been told about the dangers of the river they were camping next to and my father was told to keep guard by the river. It was first light; he had been stoking his fire. He saw the American trying to get a close-up photo of the Hippo as he surfaced his huge body out of the water. My father could not believe that the man did not run; he ran up shouting to try and get the American to move away and was trampled to death.

The new master did not want Mamma and her four children. He didn't realise that they were very good servants. I was only nine years old but I could chop wood and fetch water, tend to the goats and milk the cows. My mother had tried to tell the new master this when he came to her mud hut to tell her she would have to go. She begged him to let her stay but he told her she had too many children to feed. That was when she had the idea to send me away with the masters' things. She knew that when the master found him, he would be happy to have a servant and would give him food and clothes in return. She got one of the elders to write a letter for her telling the master what a good boy Fado was, listing all the things he could do to help even though he was just nine years old.

When all was packed and ready to be taken to the ship, Mamma put me in the crate with twelve bags of rice cakes, water and oranges. She told me to eat them sparingly and they would be enough for the journey. She showed me how to open the lid of the crate so that I could get out when no-one was about whilst he was on the ship. She told me she loved him and that one day I would have enough money to come back and see her and my brothers and sisters. I clung to my brothers and sisters and they all cried and cried.

My mother lifted me into the crate and covered me with all of the master's silk shirts then she shut the lid and pierced the top with lots of tiny holes, praying that her eldest son would arrive safely at the master's new home. She realised she had forgotten the letter. She looked around for somewhere safe to hide it, she picked up a large hard-backed book with gold trim; she couldn't read its title but remembered dusting it on the master's shelf. She placed the letter inside the sleeve of the cover at the back of the book and hoped her master would find it.

It was so dark in the crate and silent.

"I might die in here."

My tears had dried and I felt exhausted with sadness. The swaying of the crate and noise of the waves induced sleep for most of the long days.

"I am really hungry."

I woke   suddenly when the ship jolted. Rubbing my eyes to adjust to the dim light in the chest, I felt around for the food parcels Mamma had packed for me. I found the hessian bag of food and ate my way through several of the food parcels.

"Ow, my legs feel all tingly."

I tried to open the lid remembering how Mamma had told me to do it.

"I have got to get out of here and stretch my legs. I can't stay in here another minute."

Thankfully the lid opened.

"Wow, it's just like being in the master's house. There is the big red and gold chair, the four-poster bed and the huge wooden wardrobe."

I peered through the half-open lid of the chest. I could not see or hear anyone around so I decided to climb out of the chest. I lay on the floor rubbing my legs to restore the feeling in them and then managed to crawl around the boxes and pull myself up on the side of a chair.

"Just imagine what my brothers and sisters would say if they saw me sitting on the master's chair?"

I started to cry again as I thought of my long-lost family. Feeling my legs coming back to life I got off the chair. Looking into one of the boxes I found it full of mangoes.

"This is just what I need, my favourite fruit!"

I peeled the skin off with my teeth. It was ripe and juicy.

"I think I will have another!"

I devoured the delicious juicy fruit greedily. They helped to quench my thirst and hunger.

I spent days walking around the huge crate. I played games pretending that I was the master telling the servants to fetch and carry for me. I had eaten all the mangoes and my food packages. Now there was nothing left. The chest was beginning to smell as I had to go to the toilet in the corner of a big wardrobe.

"How much longer will I be in this boat? Will I survive the journey?"

I thought about my mamma, brothers, sisters and cousins, I missed them all so much. I felt lost and lonely, a tear slid down my cheek as my eyes closed and I drifted off to sleep again to dream about my beloved homeland.

I was woken with a start as my chair slid, then crashed into the boxes, then slid back again and the boxes began to topple. I was very frightened and decided the safest place to be was back in the chest with the silk shirts. I managed to push and slide myself back to the chest where I crawled inside and shut the lid. I tripped up and down in the chest for a while until all seemed to calm down and I sensed that I was floating, the air around the chest seemed cooler.

"I will have to open the chest and see what is happening!" I gasped. "Help! We are floating onto the shore."

Suddenly, there was a thud as the whole crate skidded onto the beach.

I peered out of the chest with wide terrified eyes as all of the contents of his master's house spilled out of the crate.

"What shall I do now? I can't just leave all my masters' things, what would Mama say if I did that?"

I climbed out of the chest and fell onto my knees looking across at the sea of devastation. The beach was covered with all manner of things that had fallen out of the other crates. Huge red, green and blue tractors balanced precariously on the water's edge, motorbikes looking ready to ride, boxes and containers were ripped open with their contents spilling out.

"I want my mamma!" I cried.

I knew that my master would never find me and I was all alone in a strange world. I looked out to sea and fear overtook me again. I could see a storm coming towards the beach and I could feel the wind and rain whirling up around me. I panicked as I saw a lady in a long dark coat walking across towards the crate, head down holding onto her hat with her wild auburn hair blowing across her face. With my heart beating fast and furiously, I dived back into the chest of silk shirts.

"Phew! That was a close one, how am I going to get out of here without anyone seeing me? Where am I going to go when I do get off the beach anyway?" Fado began to cry again quietly to himself.

I thought of my strong, brave father and prayed for him to guide him in what to do.

After what seemed like a lifetime I peered through the open lid again and seeing the coast was clear I climbed out.

"Oh! The wind is nearly blowing me off the beach, I must run for shelter."

I took a last look at his chest and the now wet and ruined silk shirts. Looking out to sea I could see the sailors being helped out of the wrecked ship. A group of security men waited for them on the beach with what looked like a television camera crew.

"I must get off this beach before they come looking for me."

I knew this was an irrational thought as I had not seen any sailors throughout my voyage, but I was frightened of everybody and everything, all my world had been turned upside down.

I made my way along the pebbles with a heavy heart. I struggled to climb up the beach but somehow found the strength to keep going.

"I think I should follow this fence!" I shouted to myself as the wind and rain battered against me.

A crash of thunder drove me on. Trampling through the muddy field I climbed the gate at the end into another field.

"Where am I? I can't see where I am going with the sheets of rain streaming across my face."

A hedge ran down the side of the field.

"I am going to get on my hands and knees alongside this hedge to get some shelter. Wait, there is a way through here which must have been made by an animal."

I peered into the clearing and crawled through the hedge. I kept my head down so that the twigs didn't poke in my eyes. Suddenly I felt myself falling down a hole. All was dark and black as I hit the bottom and there I stayed wet, weak and cold at the bottom of a dark hole, I put my hands in my head and cried and cried.

"Oh no, I am going to die here; wait, are those some dogs barking that I can hear?"

I managed to find my voice and cried out but it was drowned by the barking dogs, the wind and the rain.

"Is that a stick? I could try and reach it."

I grabbed it with both hands and felt myself being pulled up through the hole until I was face to face with three dogs and a lady with a leather hat holding her arms out to me. I willingly fell into them with no strength left to struggle. I could hear her soothing voice reassuring me but I did not understand what she said. I just knew that I would be safe in her arms.

Chapter 3

Hattie

Hattie was woken at seven by the phone ringing. It was her youngest daughter Ria; she always rang early to catch her mother before she went out to the horses.

"Hi, Mum, have you seen the news about the shipwreck? Seth and I are going to pop home so that we can go and see the spectacle. We couldn't believe such a thing could happen on our very own beach! Apparently someone's whole house contents were washed up. They were from Africa where we went on horseback safari."

As Hattie listened to her daughter's young enthusiastic voice, the events of yesterday came flooding back to her. The boy! Was he still sleeping next door? How could she have slept through the night when she should have been watching over him? How would she explain about the boy to her children?

"Mum, are you even listening to me? We will be home tonight. We don't have to be back at university until Monday afternoon so we can have a nice long weekend together."

Oh, Lord, thought Hattie. *I have no idea how I am going to explain about the boy, I don't even know anything about him myself!*

"OK, Ria, I have got to go now, I'll speak to you later."

"But, Mum, during the weekend, is it OK to bring Seth?" Ria was saying as Hattie put the phone down and jumped out of bed.

She had found the boy under the bed eventually last night after searching the house for him. She had contemplated sleeping in the room with him. Her own bed was so comfy and she couldn't afford to lose a night's sleep. She needed her wits around her to face the consequences of what she had done.

"Where would he be this morning? I suppose he may never have been in a bed before."

She opened his bedroom door, but he was nowhere to be seen again. As she automatically straightened up the duvet and fluffed up the pillow, she heard a muffled sound from under the bed. She bent down and there was the boy curled up in the foetal position.

"Come on, love, time to wake up."

The boy stared at her with his huge and dark frightened eyes. Hattie managed to fold her arms around his small frail body and pulled him towards her.

She pulled herself up and carried the boy downstairs where she sat him down at the table and began to prepare a wholesome farmhouse breakfast of bacon, eggs and beans.

There was a knock at the door.

"Oh, Lord, who can that be?" Hattie exclaimed out loud so that the boy recoiled in his chair. "Sorry, love, it's just that, Hattie doesn't get many people knocking at the farmhouse door. You drink your orange whilst I see who it is."

Shutting the kitchen door not wanting to have to explain about the boy at the moment, Hattie went out to the back door. It was only Sheila her yard manager bringing the dogs around

27

and wondering if Hattie was OK as she had not appeared at the stables or let the dogs out. Sheila peered suspiciously towards the kitchen door sniffing at the breakfast.

"Hattie, are you OK? It's not like you to be up without an early morning visit to the stables."

Sheila was more than an employee of Hattie; she was a good friend and the two women shared most of their ups and downs in life whilst working at the yard together.

"Yes, fine thanks," Hattie replied, "I was hungry, so I am having some breakfast, I will be out in a minute; I had a terrible time getting all the horses in last night."

"Oh, what a storm! Poor you getting all the horses in on your own. You must have been drenched!"

"Well, yes I was and exhausted, will you manage if I stay in and recover a bit this morning?"

Hattie thought it would be good to buy some time whilst she worked out what to do about the boy.

"Of course, we don't have riders until later, so I will give them all hay and skip out for now."

Hattie was half shutting the door on Sheila when there was a crash and a squeal coming from the kitchen.

"Oh no, sounds like the cat's trying to get my breakfast."

Hattie slammed the door and dashed to the kitchen. Back at the yard, Sheila expressed her concern about Hattie's odd behaviour to Rebecca.

"I've known Hattie for ten years and never known her not to come down to the stables first thing."

"Very worrying, I had a feeling someone was in the kitchen," Sheila told Rebecca about the noise she had heard when Hattie was shutting the door.

"Ooh! Maybe she has found an admirer we don't know about."

"Ha, you could be right, Rebecca, but there's not much she doesn't tell me about, so I wouldn't be surprised."

"Watch this space, I say." Rebecca went towards her horse giggling.

Sheila got on with her jobs full of speculation.

Hattie rushed back to the kitchen.

"What's going on here?"

The cat had jumped onto the table when the dogs had run in, knocking the boy's orange flying. He was terrified and jumped onto the table as well as knocking the chair over.

Hattie grabbed the boy.

"There you go, don't you be worrying about those silly dogs, all noise for nothing they are."

She felt him relax his terrified grip around her neck so she sat him back down, cleaned up the juice and then finished cooking the breakfast, crisis over. They both enjoyed the hot food. Although Fado used his fingers to scoop the food off the plate he didn't touch the bacon. Hattie realised he probably hadn't used cutlery before and maybe he didn't eat bacon wherever he had come from. The tribe she had met in Africa ate goat meat.

"Don't like bacon then? Well not to worry, we don't want you to have an upset tummy to add to your troubles."

After the pots had been cleared, Hattie took the boy back upstairs where she showed him the toilet and to her relief he did go.

"Now what can you wear?"

An old teddy caught her eye; he was sitting on the chair on the landing still wearing the shorts and tee shirt her son had dressed him in years ago. Hattie decided they would be just the right size and she was right. She remembered how difficult it was to get the clothes on her darling little boy who objected to wearing anything apart from a pair of green towelling shorts and a Thomas the Tank Engine jumper. She had got up one morning to find the clothes she had put out for him to wear on Big Ted whilst he was dressed in his favourite outfit. A tear ran down her face at the memory.

The boy stood limp whilst she dressed him.

"You'll be as right as rain in no time," she reassured him. "What will I do with him now? I really need to get out to the stables, but he seems far too weak and traumatised to go anywhere."

Hattie realised she was talking to herself but she was full of worry and could not let the boy see her concern.

"Right then, lad, let's go and raid the kids' old toy box, there will be all manner of things in there to keep you busy," she told him brightly.

The boy's eyes lit up as he saw the toy garage and the cars. A little worn looking rabbit caught her eye. Tom and it were inseparable during his short life. Tears streamed down Hattie's face. She took a deep breath as she picked up the box of toys.

She took them, some books and jigsaws back to the bedroom and he settled down to play with them.

"There, love, you have fun playing with all these toys whilst Hattie gets on with her jobs."

The boy didn't look up. Hattie was sure he couldn't understand a word she was saying. She smiled as the boy's eyes opened wider than ever as he examined the toys and books. She shut the door and decided that he was happy and safe enough to leave there whilst she went out to the stables.

"Hi, Sheila, here I am at last, feeling much better after some hot food inside me."

"Oh good, I am pleased to see you. They have all been fed and given hay but the mud is going to take a bit of getting off them."

Hattie felt guilty as she observed Sheila looking cold and wet.

"I'll tell you what, we'll have a coffee, you look frozen."

Sheila admitted she was soaked and went to find a dry coat whilst Hattie made the coffee. However really, now she was out here, she found that she couldn't wait to get back to the boy. She hurriedly groomed the ponies, got the indoor school ready for the lesson and then dashed back to the house.

Taking the stairs two at a time she called, "Here I am," as she gently opened the door to find him asleep on the bed with toys and books spilling onto the floor.

The rabbit cuddled up with him. She suppressed her tears as she ran back out to the indoor school. She taught the lesson, knowing that it wasn't one of her best as her mind was on the boy.

"Hattie, are you OK?"

Sheila was standing by the door watching her.

"Well, I feel I must have caught a chill last night."

Hattie was desperate to get back inside to the boy.

"It's six now, so you get in by the fire, I'll finish off here."

Hattie was grateful to Sheila and did not hesitate to dash off.

"I'm back," she shouted in the hope that the boy would come running to find her.

She noticed the answerphone flashing as she passed through the hall. She stopped to listen to it. There was a message from social services and they wanted to speak to her urgently. Hattie thought she had left her mobile number and was annoyed they hadn't rung on that. She checked it for missed calls and found that it had gone onto silent.

"Oh no. how did that happen?"

She pressed voicemail.

"My name is Susie Fisher. I will need to visit you as soon as possible regarding the message you left us yesterday. Please ring me on this number urgently."

Hattie checked her watch, nearly six o'clock; would they still be there if she phoned back now? Hattie dialled the number again to be greeted by the answerphone. She left them another message explaining the problem with her phone and she assured them that the boy was safe and well.

"Hello, darling."

She found him awake and ran up to him wrapping him in her arms.

"Now, my boy, we have got lots to do. My daughter is coming home. I'm not sure how I'm going to explain you to them."

The boy looked up at her with his big frightened eyes. Hattie didn't think he understood a word she said.

She jumped up as the phone rang.

"Hi, Mum, listen, Si is going to a stag do this weekend and I know it's short notice but I have decided to come to the farm. I just spoke to Ria and she says she is on her way. She was telling me about the shipwreck as I hadn't had the time to watch the news. I don't want to be left out, it'll be great fun to go and see all the debris on the beach and we might find some really interesting treasures. I'll get there around eight as I have already left work."

"Oh, Lord, what am I going to do now?"

Millie, her eldest daughter certainly wouldn't approve of her keeping the boy; she was always so sensible and well organized. She would come up with a plan and lots of scenarios if the plan was not carried out.

Hattie did want to help this boy and give him a lovely home but had no idea if the authorities would let her if she turned him over to them.

When she was a child, she used to hide the kittens in the barn so that her father wouldn't drown them. No, she must get a grip on herself; this was a boy, not a kitten and she was a grown-up who had to face the consequences of what she had done. She loved her children dearly but this was one time when she wished they were not coming to visit.

Hopefully her son wouldn't decide to arrive impromptu.

Hattie made a big shepherd's pie for everyone and decided she would explain about the boy over dinner; she had a glass of wine and whilst she was making it, it gave her some Dutch courage.

The dogs barked and she heard a car arriving. Hattie ran to the door to greet her youngest daughter Ria and her boyfriend Seth. Ria was as happy to see the dogs and cats as she was her mother; she loved the farm and all the animals especially the horses. She was enjoying her city life at university but knew that one day she would return to the life she loved.

"Mmm, something smells good, can I get a cider?"

Hattie liked the way Seth made himself at home.

She told everyone who stayed at the farm that they would have to help themselves as she often had to leave guests whilst she attended to horses.

They all sat down with their drinks and Hattie decided to approach the subject of the boy.

"Well, I have some news. I, err, I have found a boy. He was down a badger hole, he must have come from the shipwreck, but he hasn't spoken so I don't really know."

"Mum, what do you mean? Where is this boy? And why do you think he was from the shipwreck?"

"Well, he is upstairs in the Dartmoor."

The bedrooms were all named after horses and had wooden plaques on the doors from when she used to do bed and breakfast.

"He seems very weak and tired; I don't know what I am going to do with him, but at the moment I am just looking after him. I did phone social services last night. They phoned back saying they wanted to speak to me urgently."

"Have you spoken to them now?"

"Well not yet as it was too late again by the time I had finished the lessons."

"I don't know what Millie will say about this. I can see that you didn't really have a choice but to rescue him from the badger hole, but the consequences of taking him in are complicated to say the least!"

Hattie knew her daughter was right but had no time to answer as the dogs were barking again and this time it was her eldest daughter Millie at the door.

Millie rushed into the house hugging and kissing everyone whilst talking twenty to the dozen.

Hattie poured her some wine and topped up her own glass for more Dutch courage. She set about serving up the shepherd's pie and veg while Ria kept giving her looks of expectation; Millie noticed eventually and asked what was going on.

"Well, it's unbelievable really, but yesterday I found a boy down a badger hole and he is asleep up in the Dartmoor."

"Mum, you can't just take a boy in, his parents are probably going frantic. You need to report it to the authorities."

"Mum thinks he is from the crate with all the house contents of the house from Africa; with him being well, you know that colour, which means his parents will be a long way from Sidmouth."

"What has the boy got to say for himself by way of explaining what he was doing in a badger set on our farm?"

Hattie knew it would be difficult for her eldest daughter to understand that she had acted on impulse and gone into rescue mode as she had done all her life if she had seen anyone or in particular any animal in need of her help. She tried to explain that the boy was too weak and traumatised to speak or even get out of bed yet.

"Well, let's see the boy, maybe we can encourage him to talk to us."

Hattie went up to the boy's room and found him sitting up playing with the toys she had found for him. She smiled and sat on the bed talking all the time. She lifted him out of the bed as he clutched the old rabbit. She carried him downstairs. "Everything will be OK; you'll see they will love you."

Everyone was sitting around the kitchen table all talking at once. They stopped as soon as they saw her and as their eyes met the boys, he buried his head in Hattie's shoulder. Hattie sat down with him trying to reassure him that he was safe.

"Well, he sure is black," announced Seth.

"Seth, you can't say that! Poor boy, he looks shattered, Mum."

Ria looked sympathetically at him.

"Hello, love, and what is your name?"

Millie tried to approach him but he just buried his head further into Hattie's neck.

"Well, Mum, it's clear that he is indeed traumatised and needs a lot of care to bring him back to health both mentally and physically. Do you think you will have time for him with all the horses and everything else you have to do? Or are you acting irrationally, thinking about Tom maybe?"

"Millie, I can always make time for someone needy, you know that."

Hattie's eyes filled with tears at Millie's reference to Tom.

"Yes, but a boy is different from one of your rescued horses, cats or dogs."

"Millie has got a point, Mum, but you are great with kids and I am sure you'll manage."

Ria was always able to empathise with Hattie.

"The main problem is, whose boy is he? And how do we go about tracing where he came from so that we can return him safely?"

Seth was very practical when it came to sorting things out.

"I am afraid we are going to have to inform the police or the home office in the morning."

Hattie told Millie about social services. Everyone agreed with Millie's suggestion although Hattie was not sure if she really wanted to do that yet. She felt it would be better to try and get the boy well and maybe able to speak up for himself before involving the authorities. She asked Millie and Ria to go and serve the pudding as the boy was still clinging to her.

"I think your first job in the morning must be to phone social services back," Seth advised Hattie.

They all ate their rice pudding in relative silence, each of them glancing occasionally at the boy and wondering what to make of the situation. Hattie fed him and he ate greedily.

After dinner Ria was able to prize the boy from Hattie's lap and take him to play with their old box of Lego in the lounge. Hattie smiled to herself as she watched them for a moment before going to clear up and make hot drinks. Millie and Seth were obviously discussing the situation in the sun lounge.

Hattie did appreciate their concern, but didn't want to be rushed into doing something she would later regret. She had an inner sense that the boy was here to stay and there was no hurry to get him known to the public yet. However, she knew that this was one occasion that she would not be able to follow her instincts. She phoned social services back first thing. They arranged to visit her and the boy in the afternoon.

Chapter 4

Fado

The first few weeks at Hattie's were a blur. I slept most of the time and felt too weak to move. I was just grateful that Hattie was looking after me, giving me lovely food and caring for my every need in such a kind and gentle way. I didn't understand what she was saying, but her lovely smile and soothing voice were enough to get me through the traumatic time. I couldn't believe that I didn't have to tend the goats or fetch the water.

However, a part of me was very sad that I had left my beautiful homeland. Everything was so alien to me and I missed my family dreadfully. In fact, I was so traumatised that I couldn't find my voice. The language barrier didn't help.

I felt a sense of worry as Hattie's family arrived. Voices were raised and there was lots of discussion, presumably about me. I had the feeling they didn't approve of her taking me in. I think they told the police. All the family went to the beach where I had been washed ashore. Hattie carried me down. I buried my head in her neck because of all the horror I had experienced there. Hattie was drawn to a crate with things from a house; big wooden cabinets, beds and chairs. I realised these were my master's belongings. I started to cry and beat my fists on Hattie's chest in the hope that she would take me away. She saw my distress and took me off the beach.

A lady came to visit Hattie and she wanted to see me. I couldn't answer any of her questions and she kept shaking her head and looking at Hattie. I just buried my head into her jumper. Hattie had to fill in some forms. Day by day I got a little stronger and Hattie was able to take me with her to feed the chickens and collect the eggs. I helped to feed the goats. I loved them as they reminded me of home but it was strange to me that they did not give milk nor were they killed for food. They were just part of Hattie's family along with the horses, dogs, cats and chickens. She just seemed to love and care for them all.

After a few weeks I was strong enough to walk and even run a little. With the help of Hattie massaging my back I was much straighter. One day I was strong enough to meet the horses and ponies. At first I was really scared, they seemed so big; I had never been closed to one before. My people didn't have anything to do with horses. I had seen them being ridden across the Mara but they were only for the very rich. I didn't know or understand anything about Hattie's greatest passion.

She was very patient with me. I would follow her around along with the dogs, up and down the fields in and out of the stables. One day when she was grooming one of the smallest ponies, she called a Shetland, I reached up and touched the pony's long black mane. A huge smile spread across Hattie's face and she handed me a brush. That was the start of my passion. From that day on, the little pony Bubbles and I were inseparable.

Every morning I would jump out of bed and run to the field to catch Bubbles. It was a long climb up to the top where

Bubbles always liked to be with his friend Dink. One day, I got to the gate and opened my mouth to call him but to my surprise I was able to shout Bubbles! He looked up and came running down to me. Hattie came running up to me, picked me up, swung me around and hugged me; at last, I had found my voice again.

From that day Hattie began to educate me. We had to spend at least an hour every day learning new English words. I was keen to learn anything that was related to Bubbles and his care so that I could ask the stable girls for help with him when I needed it and Hattie was busy. I never had the chance to go to the school back home as I was the eldest and after my father died I needed to help with his chores. Hattie was pleased that I seemed quick to learn and could soon read and write simple sentences.

When her girls visited the farm again, Hattie seemed proud to show them how well I was doing with everything. They talked about me going to school but Hattie said I had not been officially cleared by the authorities. I did not know what that meant, other than being the reason I could not attend the school like the other children at the stables.

I had made some good friends now that I could speak. I really wished I could go with them to school as it was quite lonely for me during the day. Hattie always had lots to do. It was Bubbles that kept me happy and soon I was able to get him ready all by myself and go off riding round the fields. One of the dogs, a Lurcher named Holly, who was nearly as tall as Bubbles, always came with us. She was such a kind and gentle dog and we had formed a very good friendship right from the start. Holly didn't like to run about as much as the labs did and preferred to stay by my side as if to babysit whilst Hattie was doing jobs around the farm before I was strong enough to join her.

Now that I could speak Hattie asked me about my past life. I told her about my family and the chores I used to do every day after my father had been killed. Every time I began to talk about my family I would start to cry. Hattie would soothe me and tell me it was alright and I didn't have to go on. I did want to tell Hattie about the master and how hard my mother had to work at the big house whilst I looked after my brothers and sisters, but I couldn't as the thought of my homeland and how much I missed it   upset me so much.

Chapter 5

Hattie

"Oh, my! Was that the boy calling Bubbles down the field? Just look at that pony running to him, well I never thought I would see this day!"

Hattie sniffed and drew her sleeve across her nose as a tear escaped.

"What did you say, lad?"

"What did you say, lad?" repeated Fado.

Hattie laughed and threw her arms around the boy.

"Thank, the Lord, you can speak at last."

"You can speak at last," repeated Fado.

From that day on he began to talk; he was most enthusiastic about any words to do with horses and ponies and this thrilled Hattie. She would never have believed the poor, weak and traumatised little waif could become so strong and animated around the horses and ponies.

Hattie had become very friendly with the social worker Susie who visited regularly to monitor Fado's progress. She rang her now.

"Susie, Fado has just spoken."

"Oh, how lovely. What did he say?"

"He called out to his Shetland pony, Bubbles."

"Oh, how sweet."

"Yes and then he repeated everything I said."

"That's such a breakthrough. I'll pop around and see him tomorrow."

"OK, we'll look forward to seeing you about the boy."

Susie had been such a great help to Hattie and Fado. She could see right from the start at how good Hattie was with the boy. She applied for an emergency placement order for Fado. Hattie had been approved as a carer whilst they were trying to find out about him. Hattie had an inexplicable sense of possessiveness over the boy. She wanted to protect him from the authorities. She knew it was because of what had happened to her son. She was determined to keep hold of this boy.

They should have taken him straight into foster care. But Susie pointed out that Fado had already been so traumatised and moving him again would not be in his best interest.

One evening, when she was having five minutes of peace, Hattie picked up the Book of Africa that she had found on the beach. Whilst she was flicking through the pages admiring the brilliant wildlife photography, a slip of paper fell out of the book.

"What is this? It looks like a letter."

It was beautifully written by a black ink pen. Hattie picked up her glasses and read on.

Dear Master,

One of the elders has helped me to write this letter to you. If you remember my husband was killed whilst trying to save one of your tourists from the mouth of a hippo, the new master says he does not want me and my children because I have no man.

Please forgive me for putting my eldest son Fado in a crate and sending him across the water with your belongings. He is a good boy and can be your servant. He looks small but is very strong and can do all jobs for you. I cannot feed all my family and think this is the only thing I can do to help you and him.

Thank-you,
Favier

"This is the mother of my boy. How could she put her boy on the ship knowing she might never see him again? Much as my three might have driven me mad at times, I would never have been able to give them away like that."

Hattie read the letter over again. What should she do? Should she show it to the police or the social workers or tell her family?

One good thing, at least was that she could call the boy by his real name now instead of lad or tiny. He would be surprised in the morning when he woke up and she was calling him by his real name. She rang Ria her youngest daughter to discuss the letter.

Within an hour of putting the phone down her eldest daughter Millie was on the phone. After discussing many scenarios and weighing up the pros and cons, it was decided that they should tell George, the police officer that had been dealing with the case.

Hattie awoke early waiting for Fado to come downstairs.

"Hello, my love, come and sit down with me. I've got something to show you."

She read the letter to him.

"Want to keep Mamma's letter," he cried and cried. "I'm never going to see her again."

Fado was inconsolable.

"Yes you will. We will go to Kenya and find your mother and your family," Hattie reassured him.

He was clutching the letter to his chest. She held him close to her. Perhaps she should not have shown him the letter. How could she get him to part with it so that she could show it to the police?

"We will show the letter to the police. They can use it to help find your family."

"No! I want to keep the letter."

Fado cried even harder.

"It's OK, you will get it back," Hattie tried to reassure him.

Detective sergeant George Payne read the letter with interest and said that the pieces of the jigsaw were now starting to fit together. An ex-business man had come forward as the owner of the house contents found on the beach. He had been returning to live in the South of England after selling his estate in Kenya. George said he would try and contact the man and see if he had any idea about the boy's family.

Hattie received this news with mixed emotions. Yes, it would be good for Fado to locate his family but from the contents of the letter it seemed his mother could not care for him. Also, she had become extremely fond of the boy and did not want to lose him.

Hattie continued to teach Fado new words every day and he was soon speaking sentences. He had come a long way since those first weeks of his recovery. He seemed to have grown and that wasn't surprising by the amount he was eating. It had been difficult at first to explain his sudden appearance at the stables but now everyone loved him and they had all accepted that he was as much a part of Hattie as her beloved horses and always by her side, as were her loyal dogs. Sheila frequently questioned her.

"When will the boy's parents show up?"

Hattie had been vague about his origin and future.

"Everyone wants to know where he came from."

"Let's just say he found me. I will care for him until he can find his family."

Hattie thought that enough by way of speculation. There was much speculation amongst the others at the stables.

Everyone could see that Hattie was very fond of the boy. Pride for him exuded from her when she saw him growing in confidence with the Shetland pony and forming a bond with him. She was training him to compete in a show in the child handler class and he was showing real potential.

After a particularly busy Saturday she was settling down to a glass of wine and her favourite dinner of pasta when the phone rang.

"Is that, Hattie Gee? My name is Justin Smith; can I have a word please?"

"Yes, I am Hattie. What is this about?"

"I have been asked to pursue an enquiry about a lost boy and believe you may be able to assist me."

"In what capacity are you making this enquiry and for who?"

"I have been asked by an ex-business man from Kenya called Tristan Tomkin in my capacity as a lawyer. Look, the best thing would be for me to come around and have a chat with you."

"OK, but I am really busy during the day."

Hattie wanted to avoid the meeting in case it led to Fado being taken away.

"Yes, I am sure you are. This job is a bit of an extra for me; you see, I was in Kenya as well and knew Tristan from the expats club. Would tomorrow at eight suit you?"

Hattie felt she had to agree to this as she would have Fado in bed by this time.

Now how am I going to deal with this lawyer? I certainly don't want him having any contact with Fado at the moment. I don't know why I have just agreed to see the man. Hattie felt extremely apprehensive about the whole thing. She wondered whether she should inform George about the call.

She poured herself another glass of wine as she pondered over how to deal with the problem.

That night Hattie did not sleep well; she drifted in and out of sleep, half dreaming half reliving the experience she had on her amazing horseback safari in Kenya. The image of the huge house she had stayed in at the end of her time in the bush loomed before her and the flashback of the owner humiliating the poor woman who was taking water from the horse trough rather than walk the five-mile round trip to the water hole. The whole group had been embarrassed and upset by his action. Was this the same Tristan as Justin was working for? It seemed too much of a coincidence that they both had the same name.

Hattie went about her duties with the animals the next day somewhat subdued as she was worried about the lawyer's impending visit. She avoided people at the stables as she knew her face would tell that she was concerned about something and she didn't want to discuss it with anyone.

All too soon the day had flown past and it was seven o'clock, Fado's bath time. He did ask her if anything was wrong but she gave him a cuddle and assured him that all was well.

At eight o'clock on the dot the doorbell rang. Hattie had pictured a middle-aged balding man with glasses and rounded belly but when she opened the door she could not have been more mistaken. There on her doorstep was a tall, slim, fair-haired and very handsome man, who she guessed was in his late forties. A broad smile spread across his face as he took her hand with a strong firm grip.

Wow, I haven't experienced this tingling feeling about anyone since I had a crush on that riding instructor all those years ago!

Her whole body was alive as she struggled to speak. Justin put her at ease with his friendly banter.

"Good job, I set off early. I must have missed a turning and found myself on a green road. I had to turn up a farm track and found a farmer who knew you."

He kept hold of her hand as he was telling her all this and only let go as he stepped through the door.

"What a beautiful home you have!" he gasped as he looked up at the galleried staircase.

Chapter 6

Justin

Justin was sitting behind his desk full of unread reports and fingering his Jack Daniels, willing himself not to drink it as he knew it was wrong to be drinking at eleven in the morning, but it was his only way of coping with the enormity of what he had done.

"What is wrong with me? I should consider myself lucky to have found any sort of job back in England after being away for so many years. This remote little Devonshire town is not that different to Kenya; the people are the same country folk, they take part in illegal hunting, poaching and it's just that the consequences are not so bad for them here as they are in Kenya."

He asked himself for the thousandth time.

"Why, oh why, did I get drawn into that sordid world in Kenya?"

He had been ticking along very nicely with his simple cases of poor folk breaking the laws out there. His wife and three beautiful children were happy and healthy if not as well off as some of their expat friends. It was sheer greed and jealousy that had made him go along with the idea. His wife had been asking him for money to get the children into this club and that he had been jealous of the rich landowners who wanted for nothing in his beloved Mara.

He had agreed to put the poor people that he had convicted to work on the drugs farm in the most appalling conditions and because of this, he had lost everything. When his wife Annette found out, she took herself and their three children back to live with her parents in Austria and told him she never wanted to see him again.

The phone rang just as Justin had drained his glass.

"Hi, Justin, my dear fellow, long time no hear, how are you? Settling down to the homeland again? Well, I am back here myself, you know!"

"Tristan, what a shock. I didn't realise you were in England. Err, how did you track me down?"

"Well, I am in a spot of bother, old chap, and the local police recommended you. I couldn't believe it, man, you being my long-lost friend."

"What sort of bother are you in?"

"Well, a great deal as it happens. You see, all the contents of my house were shipwrecked. You probably heard about it as it was on the coast near you.

"Yes, the beach where I live was covered in the debris from the ship."

"That's right and the problem is that a child was found amongst my belongings and now this crazy woman has him and she has found a letter from his mother hidden inside one of my books."

"I am with you so far but not sure what I can do to help."

"The police and social workers are involved. You know what a pain they can be? Not that we had to put up with them in Kenya! But honestly, I cannot have this getting out in public."

"Have you done something wrong regarding this child?"

"Oh no, I wouldn't say that. Not exactly. I don't even know the child. His mother was just one of the thousand workers I had on the estate. The trouble is, I have been labelled as the connection in finding the child's origins."

"I see. Well, this obviously needs looking into. I will go and see the crazy woman who has taken him in and find out what her take is on the child. I will report back as soon as I have some info."

"Well done, old boy. I will see you right for this, I am very grateful."

Justin was shocked at the story from his old neighbour Tristan. It was ironic that this man was now seeking his help when he had such a hold on him in Kenya. The drugs farms were his business, but of course he never got his hands dirty over it. No-one even suspected his involvement.

Justin realised he should have put the phone down and had nothing to do with the man and his problem as he called it, but something in his better nature made him pursue it. The poor boy, what must he have gone through? Pushed into a ship as a stowaway and then for the ship and its contents to be washed ashore, it didn't bear him to think about that. He was also intrigued to know who this crazy woman was to have taken the boy in.

He didn't hesitate to phone the police.

"Hello, it's Justin Smith here. I have been asked to get involved in the case of a stowaway."

"I'll put you through to George. He is dealing with the case."

Chief Inspector George Payne filled him in with all the details since the boy's discovery. The case sounded intriguing. Justin was quite excited about the prospect of meeting the boy and the crazy lady named Hattie.

Justin had been trying to contact Hattie for a few days, he had rung the landline and emailed her without success. He was the sort of person who liked to get on with things once he put his mind to it and it annoyed him when he could not get immediate results, which is what made him so good at his job. Clients loved the way he got results without delay. He rang George again to see if he had a mobile number for Hattie. Fortunately, he did and he also apologised to Justin for not giving it before as he had found it the only successful method of contacting Hattie.

It was Saturday evening before Justin had a minute to ring the mobile and although he knew it was rather an unofficial time to ring, he decided to give it a try.

"Hello, my name is Justin Smith. I am a lawyer and wondered if you could spare a moment of your time?"

Justin was pleasantly surprised by the conversation. Hattie had sounded a little off hand at first by the invasive call but she soon seemed to warm to him and agreed to see him the next evening even though it was a Sunday. He would have preferred to have met the boy but respected her protective attitude and he was sure he could meet him on another occasion when he had gained Hattie's trust.

Justin was pleasantly surprised when an attractive brunette with a very characterful face opened the door of her beautiful hexagon-shaped farmhouse with its impressive view of the sea. He was aware of holding on to her hand rather longer than necessary with his handshake as his brown eyes met her deep dark ones. He laughed nervously as he told her about the difficulty he had finding the farm as he had gone straight past the private road up the typical Devon lane with its high hedges and got completely disorientated. He babbled on telling her that he had called in at Badgers Rest and they had put him right. She nodded in recognition of this and showed him into the lounge with its big bay window highlighting the panoramic views surrounding the house which he admired, lost for words.

"Would you like to join me in having a glass of wine?"

He was instantly put at ease by the warmth exuding from this special lady and he accepted her offer.

A couple of hours flew past as Hattie told Justin her extraordinary life story and how she had come to find the boy. She told him that she had been on a horseback safari in Kenya and fallen in love with the beloved country.

"Oh, I'm sorry, but it's past my bedtime," yawned Hattie.

"So sorry, I didn't realize the time."

Justin jumped up.

"Time just flies by when you're in good company."

Justin reluctantly left the intriguing lady telling her he would be in touch again soon.

Driving home on a high with his music playing loudly, it suddenly dawned on him that he hadn't asked any of the questions he should have had.

"Tristan is not going to be happy that I haven't found out half the things he wanted me to."

Justin turned down the music and realised he would have to avoid Tristan until he had seen Hattie again. He would have to ring her again tomorrow and invite her to his home where the office was, so that they could conduct a more formal meeting.

"Tristan wants me to somehow stop Hattie from pursuing the boy's origins and his connection. Also, I fear the consequences of the boy going back to his roots as it may inadvertently affect me and my position. If the reason I left Kenya became common knowledge, I may well end up in court myself!"

Justin's mood had changed as he drove into his drive. He was full of worry and concern.

"I need to ring Hattie and make another appointment to see her as soon as possible."

Justin's head was in turmoil as he climbed into bed with a feeling of excitement at the thought of seeing Hattie again.

Justin was woken up at 7:30 a.m. by the phone ringing.

"Hi, I hope I didn't wake you?"

"No of course not, it's lovely to hear from you."

"Well, I realised that I hadn't told you that I have had something on my mind in connection with the boy and my trip to Kenya."

Justin dreaded what was coming next. His worst fear was that Hattie had already connected the boy with Tristan.

"Well, there were a few things I forgot to clarify with you actually. Would it be possible to pop round again?"

"Oh yes, better than me rattling on over the phone when you probably haven't even had your breakfast yet; would tonight at eight suit you?"

"Yes, that would be fine, see you at eight."

Justin replaced the phone with a sigh of relief. He would ring Tristan when he got back later this evening and not answer the phone if he rang today. He would make sure he behaved in a more business-like manner at his next meeting with Hattie so that he could concentrate on carrying out Tristan's request.

Chapter 7

Hattie

As Hattie was dialling Justin's number, she felt the same tingling feeling inside her that she had experienced last night. I hope I don't seem too pushy ringing him at 7:30 a.m. in the morning. I have to get this worry off my mind or I will never get a peaceful night's sleep again and Lord knows I need my sleep!

After she had finished her call to Justin, Hattie felt both relieved and excited. The prospect of seeing him again so soon made her smile to herself.

However, she must focus on what she had to tell him. Hattie could not get the image of the man she had met on her horseback safari out of her head.

She recalled the time when they were riding on his estate and had come across a woman with a baby tied to her back and a toddler at her feet. She was filling her water butt from the animal drinking trough.

"Oi!" shouted Tristan, startling the poor woman.

He then began to shout at her in Swahili; she dropped the water butt and fled.

He turned to us smirking that he had told her to walk the five-mile trip to the watering hole and not steal from his animals. Most of us took an instant dislike to him, remembered Hattie. If he has anything to do with the boy, then I will fight him all the way she promised herself.

The day flew by with all the stable duties and riders to teach and take out. Hattie still had to find time to teach Fado. She loved having the opportunity to get back into her teaching. When she had first arrived in Devon, supply teaching was her main source of income. She and Ria would get up at the crack of dawn to do the horses before going off to their respective schools. In the evening she would teach riding. Hattie often wondered now how on earth she had coped with all the work, but the riding school was not as big then as it was now. She was a few years younger and had more energy as well.

"Come on, lad, time to put Bubbles away and in for your lessons."

Hattie knew what the reply would be from Fado.

"But I haven't finished his jumping lesson, please just five more minutes!"

There was always some excuse not to leave his pony.

"You can carry on with the jumping tomorrow, I want to get in today, and you need an early night, now come on."

"OK, but will you promise to come and watch Bubbles jumping tomorrow?"

"Yes I will, now you have got ten seconds to put him away, one, two…"

Fado loved it when Hattie counted to get him speeding up. He did enjoy his lessons with her and was very keen to learn. He wanted to be able to read all the magazines and books that Hattie had on horses but still found the words too hard. He loved it when Hattie read them to him at bedtime.

Hattie was aware that she was rushing through the day with nervous energy in anticipation of Justin's visit. There was so much to fit in to a day and no time to sit and think. Every minute was taken up, if she could just get half an hour before he came to compose herself. I need to tell him about Tristan and ask him if it could possibly be the same guy he knows. If it is, then Justin is working for a very unpleasant character in my opinion. Hattie had lost track of the counting when Fado appeared at her side.

"You didn't even get past five that time, Hattie, and I'm all done and ready to go. Can you teach me how to read the pony club magazine today?"

"Oh, Fado, there's more to learn in life than pony club magazines, you know."

"Yes, but all the girls at the stables were saying that we were in it because we had got lots of badges and I want to see that."

"OK, we'll see how we get on with number work first."

Hattie had wanted to cut the lesson short today so that she could get on with tea and bedtime. Maybe she could quickly hide the pony club magazine.

As it turned out, Fado was quick to learn his number work and there was time to look at the magazine.

After a quick tea of sausage and beans it was bath and bedtime.

"Great. I have time for a glass of wine and to get my thoughts together. Oh bother, that's my mobile."

Hattie ran to fetch her mobile off the lounge table.

"Hello, oh, hi, Ria, how are you?"

Hattie thought it was bad timing that her youngest daughter should ring but could not do anything about it. She listened to all the latest dramas of university life.

"Ria, do you remember the owner of the safari park we rode in when we went to Kenya?"

"Yes, that awful snooty man who kept making racist comments, why?"

Hattie had not meant to talk to Ria about Justin, but found herself unveiling the whole story.

"Well, Mum, be careful; sounds to me like you quite fancy this Justin bloke, but if he's anything to do with that Tristan, he won't be a very nice character."

Ria had told Hattie what she did not want to hear, but had thought it herself. She resolved not to be so friendly towards her visitor tonight. She must be more business-like.

The doorbell rang and her heart began to flutter.

Chapter 8

Fado

Life was getting better daily and the effect of the traumatic journey that had brought me to the farm was beginning to fade. I have grown very close to Hattie and am beginning to overcome my fears on the farm.

When Hattie first took me to meet the horses I was terrified. The animals' huge heads and those big, bright almond-shaped eyes seemed to follow me around the stables wherever I went. Hattie tried to reassure me that they were gentle giants and would not intentionally harm me. I did not have the words to explain to her that where I came from, animals this size were to be feared and kept well away from. It was not very helpful that the naughty little pony Dinky turned his head too quickly and nearly knocked me flying! Hattie caught him just in time before I fell onto a pile of horse dung.

Hattie was completely at one with her horses and it was watching her work with them that made me feel less anxious. When she was training a young horse or a new one to the yard, Hattie would have him or her working with her in no time. They would go into the indoor school. Hattie would put a special head collar on the horse with a long rope attached.

First, she would ask the horse to walk a certain distance behind her. If she thought the horse was getting too close and invading her space, she would turn, shake the rope and ask him to back up. Then they would set off again. Eventually, the horse was licking, chewing its ears, twitching and waiting for Hattie to give the next instruction. Finally, Hattie would take the had collar off and swish the rope sending the horse off running around the school. Soon the horse would stop dead and turn to look at Hattie. She would turn her back to the horse. Fado never ceased to find the next bit amazing. In fact, it made him feel choked up with emotion. After a few minutes of the horse watching Hattie, he would walk up to her and nuzzle her shoulder. Hattie would turn, rub him, smile and tell him he was a very good boy. Hattie called this 'join up'. She told Fado that the horse and her now had the greatest of respect for each other. The horse now considered her the herd leader. I grew to love my pony Bubbles and he became my best friend and companion. Even the other stable kids were surprised at the things Bubbles and I could achieve. They had just seen him as a cheeky little pony who had bucked them off plenty of times when they had tried to make him do some work.

I knew that Hattie worried about the authorities interfering in her decision to care for me. Even more worrying though, was a conversation I overheard of Hattie on the phone to someone when she mentioned the name Tristan. Fado knew this to be the name of his father's boss man and the man who had told his mother that she would have to leave her home as she was not wanted by the new boss. It was his crate I had been put in to travel across the seas.

I did not mention anything to Hattie about the phone call I had listened to, as I knew I should have been asleep in bed. I gathered that someone connected to Tristan was going to visit Hattie and I planned to get up and hide somewhere so that I could overhear the conversation.

I spent the day training my pony for the competition tomorrow. I washed his mane, tail and made his coat shiny with brushing.

"There you go, my little beauty, I think we are all ready to win the show now."

I kissed Bubbles on the nose and was putting him back in the barn when Sheila called.

"Leave him on the yard, Fado. I have to wash Dinky and he will behave better with his friend Bubbles beside him. Want to help me? You are the expert – just look at Bubbles, he is sparkling!"

"Yes, please; I love making them shine for the show. Do you think me and Bubbles will have a chance in the child handler class?"

"Of course, you will; you just need to be confident and you will be up there with the rosettes."

Fado couldn't wait to get his first rosette, but he was nervous about showing Bubbles in front of lots of people at a big show.

On the morning of the show the yard was a hive of activity at the crack of dawn with all the girls and boys getting the horses and ponies ready to go. Hattie made feeds for them all and told everyone to let the ponies have a bit of peace with their hay and feed whilst they loaded the lorry with all their tack and the hay nets.

At last, all horses and ponies were in the lorry and they were off. The showground was already buzzing with people riding and leading their horses and ponies to and from the show rings.   Lorries and trailers lined the hedge and they pulled up beside them.

"Hattie, my heart's beating very fast."

"That's good, love, helps you do well in the show if the adrenaline is flowing!"

Fado got Bubbles out of the lorry, brushed him and painted his hooves with oil to make them shine.

Hattie applied baby oil to his mane and tail to make them shine. She straightened Fado's tie and took a photo of them with a look of real pride on her face. They walked to the show ring together.

"Just remember all you have been practicing and don't get distracted by anyone else in the ring."

As soon as Fado entered the ring and he saw the judge smile at him, he relaxed and said to Bubbles, "Bubbles, we're going to win this!"

When it came to his turn to show Bubbles he walked out to the judge with confidence, smiled and said, "Good morning, sir."

The judge smiled and asked him a few questions about Bubbles before telling him to go and do a little show. Fado trotted Bubbles in a figure of eight and then stood him at a square halt in front of the judge. Bubbles behaved beautifully throughout. Fado went back to his place in the line and looked across to where Hattie was watching him; she was clapping and shouting, 'BRILLIANT.'

I felt very proud of myself and Bubbles.

The judge asked all the children to walk round whilst the steward went to fetch the rosettes.

I kept an eye on the judge as I walked round and then the best thing happened! The steward was walking towards him asking him to come and line up next to him. I couldn't believe what was happening until five more children were asked to stand next to him with their ponies and the other competitors looked rather disappointed with their heads down and left the ring.

Hattie and all the stable kids were clapping and cheering at the side of the ring as I was presented with a blue rosette and a silver cup. The judge congratulated me telling me that it was obvious I had a very good relationship with my pony.

The six children were asked to do a lap of honour. I was struggling to keep up with Bubbles in the lead whilst carrying his cup and rosette. Suddenly Bubbles heard his friend Dinky who was competing in the next ring.

"Neigh!" shouted Dinky.

Bubbles neighed back and then he was off, forgetting he had poor me at the end of his lead rein. I held on as Bubbles pulled me towards the rope dividing the show rings and then he ducked right under it leaving me caught up in the rope. Bubbles and Dinky were oblivious of the mayhem they had caused as they were happily reunited. Hattie ran to Fado who was slumped over the rope, his arm dangling awkwardly on the grass. When Hattie scooped him up into her arms, she noticed to her horror that his arm looked quite misshapen. When she touched it, he screamed in pain. She called to Sheila that she was going to have to take him to hospital. Sheila assured her she could manage things at the show whilst they were at the hospital.

"Is Bubbles OK?" murmured Fado as she put him in the car.

"Yes, love, he is fine, the naughty boy; now, we will soon have you better when the doctor has mended your arm."

When they arrived in casualty Hattie realised they were in trouble.

"What is his full name and date of birth?"

The admin nurse waited for Hattie to reply.

Chapter 9

Justin

Justin spent the drive to Hattie's going over what he was going to say when he got there.

I just need to keep focused, he thought to himself as he gripped the steering wheel and gritted his teeth.

"I have to remember that Tristan must keep out of the public eye at all costs."

What they had both been a part of in Kenya was shameful. If it became apparent that the boy Hattie had rescued was indeed from Tristan's estate, then questions would be asked about his life and the whereabouts of his family.

The problem Justin had was the impact Hattie had made on him. He hadn't been able to get her out of his mind. He admired her sheer strength of character. The passion she had for her work and for all things living melted his heart. He had been so lonely since his wife and family had left him and although he was now able to Skype his children, he desperately missed not having any physical contact. He was naturally a tactile person and needed warmth and compassion in his life. Giving them a cuddle, their hair and a goodnight kiss were the things he longed for. His imagination ran away with him as he thought of holding Hattie close to him.

The minute Hattie opened the door his resolve started to fade. He held onto her hand rather too long as she welcomed him into her home.

"Hi, how are you? The weather has been awful again, hasn't it? Or don't you notice it so much sitting behind your desk?"

"Well, I do get out of my cupboard sometimes! But you must find it very difficult. I don't know how you do it, having to battle with the elements."

"Having horses is not for lovers of fair weather, that's for sure. Now let's go and sit by the fire with a glass of wine. I have something very important to tell you."

Justin followed Hattie into the lounge where they sat down in front of the log fire. He knew that it would take all his strength not to get lulled into a false sense of security as he sank into the comfy leather chair with its warm furry throw.

"Now, this guy, Tristan, is giving me sleepless nights. If it's the same guy as my daughter and I had the misfortune to meet on our horseback safari in Kenya then I don't want the boy having anything to do with him. No, in fact, I want you to make it your job to keep him right out of our lives!"

Justin was shocked to hear Hattie's obvious dislike of Tristan and intrigued to know why she had formed this opinion of him.

"How did you meet Tristan? Was he riding on your holiday? The Tristan I know didn't particularly like horses, although, I think he used to ride one until he had a bad fall. The horse bolted with him when a buffalo chased them and Tristan came off and nearly got trampled by all accounts. He never rode again."

"Well, that would serve him right if it's the same bloke I met. He was riding then, showing us around his estate. Boasting more like. I'm not surprised the horse chucked him off; he had no respect. He was trying the jumps on his cross-country course."

"Because he was holding his reins too tight, the horse refused and he whacked the poor thing so hard with his whip, we all gasped and turned away."

Justin listened intently to the damning of Tristan's character. He only knew him socially from the expats club and had not had too much contact with him when he was dealing with the trafficking of prisoners to the drugs farm. He would have to think very carefully how to comment on Hattie's bad report of Tristan.

"Well, Hattie, the Tristan you met certainly does not sound like a very pleasant person."

"You can see why I wouldn't want anything to do with him and I certainly would not let him near the boy."

"Ah! Now that's where you and him will agree. You see, Tristan has told me that he has severed all his ties with Kenya and is trying to make a new life for himself in England. He really would have no place for the boy in his new life and would prefer it not to be known that he ever had any connection with him."

"I bet he doesn't! He is probably ashamed of himself for ever having his slaves doing all his hard work."

"Yes, I know it sounds a terrible life. However, life is very different out there and Fado's family would have been glad of the work as many of his friends and relatives would be very poor with no jobs at all."

"Well, that's a maybe, but the point is, the authorities would like to find Fado's origins. What are we going to do?"

"I think we have to play the system. We don't have to reveal to the authorities anything about our connection with Tristan. We could go back to Tristan's old estate and ask the new owners if they have any idea what happened to Fado's family."

"I think that is a very good idea, Justin. Fado would love to find his family, even though he wants to stay here with me."

"I am sure the authorities would allow that, but they will want to make it official with the permission of his family."

"I understand that and am prepared to travel to Kenya and meet his family."

"I can help with all the legal side of things. Just to make it clear then, I will tell Tristan that we both agree not to have him connected with the boy."

"The sooner you tell him that, the better I would be as far as I am concerned."

Justin finished his wine and bid goodnight to Hattie. He realised he was dealing with a very strong and determined character. Part of him thought it better not to get involved, but his heart ruled his head and made him realise he would do anything to help her.

******

Hattie had felt herself get heat up at the very mention of that horrible man Tristan. She hoped she had made it quite clear to Justin that she wanted nothing to do with the man.

"I think that police inspector George needs a call from me tomorrow. I want to tell him that he is barking up the wrong tree with Tristan's connection and the boy. Put him right off the scent," she said out loud to herself.

******

Justin was looking forward to meeting up with Tristan and telling him that there was nothing to worry about regarding Hattie and the boy.

Justin had a restless night dreaming about Hattie and her horses. He woke early.

"That woman has got right under my skin. I have my work to do and mixing work with pleasure is never a good idea."

Justin felt he would like to separate the work from the pleasure and get to know Hattie better. There was one thing preventing him from doing this. If Hattie ever found out the real reason he had to leave Kenya and the reason he had lost his wife and children, he was sure that she would not want anything to do with him.

Justin got straight on the phone to Tristan after breakfast.

"Morning, Tristan, how are you on this fine autumn morning?"

"I'll be all the better for hearing you have good news for me, my old boy."

"Well, lucky for you then, that I have."

"Excellent, so you're telling me that the crazy woman does not connect me to the boy she found?"

Justin objected to Tristan calling Hattie a crazy woman, but decided not to say anything for fear of betraying his feelings for her. He told Tristan that Hattie did not want the boy to be taken from her and as a result she did not want to

70

meet up with anyone from his past. He did not tell Tristan about Hattie's stories of him from her encounters with him on her holiday. None of it was really relevant.

He also realised that he needed to sever his ties with Tristan if he had any hope of a relationship with Hattie.

Chapter 10

Hattie

Hattie panicked and drew Fado closer to her. How was she going to explain that she had no idea of Fado's full name or date of birth? Fado cried out in pain as she held him tight. She threw her free arm as a gesture of desperation to the nurse.

"Please can you just give him something for the pain? We can fill in the paperwork when he's more comfortable."

The nurse observed the boy flinching when Hattie threw her arm up.

"Yes, we can do that. Is he allergic to anything?"

Hattie tried not to hesitate in her answer or look anxious.

"No, not that he has had any serious illness or accident before."

"Well, here is some nice strawberry medicine to make you feel better, love."

Hattie realised she had to do something quickly to buy some time. She would have to make up a date of birth and a surname. To her relief her mobile rang.

"Do you mind if I take this, it's my daughter and she doesn't know about the accident."

"OK, can you just go through that door please where mobiles are allowed."

Hattie picked up Fado, went out of the door and out of earshot of the nurse.

"Ria, what good timing, we are in the hospital. Fado has broken his arm."

"Oh no, poor lad, how did it happen?"

Hattie explained briefly about the show but her real concern was how to handle the form filling.

"What shall I do? I have no idea what his date of birth or second name is."

"Mum, just make up the birth date; perhaps the day you found him and you know from that letter he is nine. Give him your surname."

"Oh thanks, Ria, you always know how to cope in a crisis. Can you come home for the weekend and give me a hand looking after Fado?"

"Yes, I will see you on Friday. Don't worry, everything will be fine."

Feeling much better, Hattie took Fado back in to see the nurse and gave her the information she needed. A man was sitting next to the nurse.

"Good afternoon, Mrs Gee. I'm Mr Patterson, a social worker."

"Oh!" Was all that Hattie could manage to say.

"We're a little concerned about this young man."

Mr Patterson put his hand on Fado's back and smiled at him.

"Well, it was just a freak accident with his pony Bubbles." Hattie sounded defensive as she drew Fado closer to her chest.

"Yes, we're aware of the cause of his broken arm, but he has other scarring on the arm and legs."

Hattie had noticed some scars on Fado's arms and legs. When she had asked him about them, he said they were from the thorn trees in the bush back home. He used to pick the fruits from the trees but they had sharp thorns which would cut his skin. How could she explain this to the social worker?

"He's a typical boy always climbing trees; we live on a farm."

"I see," said Mr Patterson, "and his date of birth?"

"25th October 2008."

"What did you say his full name was?" the nurse asked as she checked her notes.

"Fado Favier."

Hattie gave the name she had read on the letter from his mother.

"I see, can you tell me what if any relation you are to the boy?" the nurse asked this question leaning forward on her chair and staring intensely at Hattie.

"Well, I'm his, err, guardian of course."

Hattie couldn't help the irritation in her voice.

"His social worker is called Susie Walker; if you want to speak to her, I'll give you her phone number. Now, please can he have an X-ray, we need to help him."

"She's on holiday, I'm over seeing her cases at the moment," Mr Patterson informed Hattie. "I'll let her know about this incident when she returns."

Hattie took an instant dislike to Mr Patterson; she would have to ring Susie as soon as possible.

Mr Patterson nodded at the nurse and left them.

"Wait over there for the doctor, please." The nurse pointed to a cubicle with a bed and a chair.

Hattie felt really hot and red in the face. By the time the doctor came she was sweating.

They were sent for an X-ray which showed that Fado's forearm had a clean break. Two hours later they were on their way home with Fado's arm in plaster.

"When will I be able to ride again? Fado asked the doctor.

"I am afraid you will have to wait a few weeks', young lad. Your bones need to heal first."

The doctor smiled at Hattie and told her it was important that Fado restrained his activities until the bones knit together. However, he had also reassured her that young bones do heal quickly. Fado was most upset that he would not be allowed to ride but asked Hattie if he could still help groom and do any jobs he could at the stables with one hand. Hattie assured him he would be able to help. She smiled to herself as she remembered the poor and frightened little boy she had rescued and how confident he was now around the stables.

When they arrived home, Hattie put on a DVD for Fado and told him to stay in whilst she went to make sure all was well at the stables. Everyone was really concerned about Fado and Hattie reassured them he was fine although not happy that he could not ride for a while. When she went back to the house the phone was ringing.

"Hi, Mum, how is Fado? Ria told me he had broken his arm."

"Yes he has, but he is ok, it was worrying at the time. Naughty Bubbles running off with him. He has forgiven him though, especially as he won his class at the show."

"Oh, that's a relief then. I can come home for the weekend and see him. Ria is coming on her own, isn't she? So, it will be all us girls together apart from Fado of course."

"OK, looking forward to seeing you."

Hattie loved having the girls' home with her. Even better it would be if her son would visit more often. *No good dwelling on what's not to be,* she thought. She told Fado about their visit.

"Yippee, will they take me to the toy shop again? I would like to get another pony. I saw one that looked just like Bubbles."

"I don't know about that, Fado, you mustn't expect presents all the time. We don't want everyone thinking you are spoilt."

It was lovely how the girls had taken to Fado and really did enjoy spoiling him when they came home.

Hattie was ready for bed shortly after settling Fado. It had been quite a day. Just as she was settling the dogs down the phone rang.

"Hello, Hattie, its George here. Sorry to bother you at this hour but I thought you needed to know that I had a call from the social workers today."

Hattie's hand began to shake.

"What about?"

"Well, the hospital rang the office saying a boy was brought in with a broken arm and the person with him seemed hesitant about his full name and date of birth. They asked me to look into it. Was it you, Hattie?"

"Yes, it was us. I hope you told them that it is none of their business."

"I haven't told them anything. How is the boy, anyway?"

"He is OK now, but he did have a bit of an accident and broke his arm."

"Oh dear, poor lad. I would seek advice from that solicitor chap if I was you. I think you will find that the welfare officer may be in touch with you."

"Okay, I'll ring him tomorrow."

Hattie rang Susie her key social worker for Fado.

"Well, hello stranger, I thought you had left the planet as I haven't heard from you in ages. I'm on holiday at the moment. Is there a problem?"

"I know and I'm really sorry I haven't been in touch; life is just too hectic and I don't know where the days go!"

Hattie did feel bad about not ringing Susie as she had become a good friend. The truth was that since she had met Justin, she didn't want to talk to her friends in case they noticed a change in her. She was shocked at her feelings for him and felt a bit embarrassed not knowing what to do about them.

"I suppose you heard about our visit to the hospital after Fado's accident at the show."

"Yes, it was brought to my attention, even though I wasn't really supposed to be taking work calls. I hear Mr Patterson was sent to the hospital. He hasn't been with us long and is not known for his bed-side manner."

"They're not going to try and take Fado away, are they?"

Hattie couldn't keep the panic out of her voice.

"You may have to ask the advice of your solicitor friend."

Susie knew this was a difficult situation. She didn't want to worry Hattie, but making up the date of birth and surname hadn't helped them at all!

"I'll ring him as soon as possible, thanks for your help, Susie."

"I'll have a meeting with Mr Patterson when I return to the office next week."

Susie had grown very fond of Hattie and Fado and would do all she could to keep them together.

As soon as Susie put the phone down Hattie rang Justin.

"Hi, how are you?"

"All the better for hearing your lovely voice." Justin sounded on good form.

"I'm afraid I've got myself in a spot of bother."

Hattie couldn't hide the panic in her voice from Justin.

"Oh dear, whatever has happened?"

Hattie related the story of the broken arm and the hospital visit.

"There's no denying that this is a tricky situation, not helped by the fact that you didn't explain Fado's circumstances in the first place!"

"I know that now, Justin, but I just panicked."

Hattie was near to tears.

"OK, how about I come over tomorrow evening when Fado has gone to bed and we'll discuss a strategy for dealing with this?"

"Thanks, Justin, see you tomorrow."

Hattie felt relieved that both Justin and Susie seemed sympathetic towards her predicament. The next morning, she got up really early to feed the horses before going shopping.

Fado finished his breakfast and was ready to leave by the time she got in. They were both looking forward to seeing the girls.

Fado and Hattie arrived back with the shopping to find a car waiting in the drive. It was Mr Patterson with the nurse and George the policeman. Hattie wanted to turn around and drive away. Instead, she texted Justin asking him to come now as it was urgent. Mr Patterson and the nurse got out of the car.

"What's that man from the hospital doing here, Hattie? I didn't like him."

Fado looked worried.

"I don't know, Fado, but I'll sort it out. You get the shopping in. The girls will be here in a minute."

"Hello, Mrs Gee, hopefully it's convenient to talk, may we come in?"

The nurse looked Fado up and down as he was using his good arm to support the box of shopping.

"I haven't got much time actually as I'm expecting my daughters any minute, but you'd better come in I suppose." They all went into the farm house whilst Fado got the shopping from the car.

Hattie showed them into the breakfast room.

They sat down at the table whilst Hattie picked up the piles of books and papers. She put them down at the other end of the long farmhouse wooden table. Nervously looking round to see if there was any other mess she could clear away, she asked if they'd like a drink.

"No thanks," they both replied in unison.

"You may have gathered that we're concerned about the boy, Fado, during your hospital visit."

Mr Patterson had put his glasses on and was opening his file.

"I can assure you that Fado is very well cared for and happy! He had a freak accident with his pony as I explained to the nurse at the time."

Hattie felt her face getting hot and red.

"Hi, Mum, hi, Fado, how's your broken arm? Can I be first to sign your plaster?"

Ria burst into the room.

"Ooh, yes please. Can you draw a picture of Bubbles on it for me please?" Fado called back to her from the kitchen where he was putting the shopping away.

"Ha ha! I thought you would have had enough of Bubbles by now!"

"No, it wasn't his fault that he wanted to get to his best friend," Fado told Ria.

Hattie turned to Mr Patterson and the nurse.

"I'm sorry, but this isn't the best time; don't you usually make an appointment?"

"No, we don't have to when we feel the matter is urgent." Mr Patterson replied gravely.

George looked uncomfortable. He was a good friend of Hattie.

"Look, Hattie, we just need to clear a few things up here, that's all."

The doorbell rang and Fado ran to answer it.

"Hattie, Justin's here," he called from the hallway.

"I'll put the kettle on," Ria said.

She didn't seem to have noticed the two people sitting at the breakfast table.

Justin went straight up to Mr Patterson and offered his hand to shake.

"Good evening, Mr Patterson, we have met on the Mary Thompson case, if you remember."

Hattie was so pleased to see Justin who turned to her and winked. Hattie observed Mr Patterson relaxing as he and

Justin discussed the case. She noticed the nurse discreetly taking a look at her watch and stifling a yawn.

"Oh, sorry, I didn't notice you three there. Would you like some tea?"

Ria was used to random people turning up at the farm. Hattie liked to have an open house. People she knew would pop in if they had a problem. Hattie, being a woman of wisdom and a good listener was always surrounded by people.

"Hi, everyone, I'm here, traffic was dreadful."

Millie burst into the hall. Fado ran up to her throwing his good arm around her leg.

"Hi, Justin, Mum, Ria."

Millie kissed everyone and then stopped dead in her tracks as she saw the two people sitting at the table.

"What's happened, Mum, has there been an accident?"

"No, love, this is Mr Patterson, the social worker with the nurse from the hospital, and you know, George, of course."

Millie looked puzzled.

"What about Susie? Isn't she Fado's social worker?"

"Yes, she's been away," Mr Patterson told Millie.

Justin was the first to speak after an awkward moment.

"As you can see, this is a very happy and busy household. Can I suggest Susie makes an appointment to come back another day when it is a bit quieter?"

"Yes, I think that may well be what I'll have to do. She's returning to work from her holiday next week. I'll advise her about this situation and she'll be in touch as soon as possible."

Fado opened the door and smiled at them as they left.

"Thanks, Justin, I don't know what I would have done without you here."

Hattie gave Justin a hug.

"Mum, you could be done for fraud!" Millie exclaimed.

"Millie, don't upset Mum anymore. We must be able to sort this out."

"Susie is going to speak to them explaining the situation." Hattie told them about her conversation with Susie.

"Good job you made friends with Susie, she's a great help." Millie pointed.

"What do you think will happen now, Justin?" Ria asked.

"It's a tricky one," Justin admitted.

"But I don't think it was altogether a bad thing with them turning up today."

"Why not? I thought it was terrible." Hattie said throwing her hands across the room.

"I mean, it was just chaos!"

"No, Hattie, it was just a normal and happy family household and that was good for them to observe."

"I'll give Susie a ring again tomorrow and tell her what happened, hopefully she'll be here next time they come," Hattie told everyone.

"Good idea, now let's have a glass of wine to calm our nerves after that ordeal."

Millie was opening the fridge door.

"Fado, I've bought you some DVDs."

Ria fished them out of the bag and handed them to Fado.

"Wow, Ria, can I watch one now, Hattie?"

"Of course, I'll call you when dinner is ready."

Hattie was relieved that her household was returning to normality.

"Well, I'd better be getting back."

Justin thought it diplomatic to leave Hattie to catch up with her daughters.

"Are you sure?" Hattie didn't really want to Justin to leave.

"Yes, I've things to attend to that I was in the middle of when I got your text."

"Of course, you must get back to them. I'm so grateful to you for dropping everything and coming here. I think it was a great help."

"No problem, any time."

Justin gave Hattie a kiss on the cheek before turning towards the door. Hattie rushed after him hoping the girls wouldn't see her blushing. When she returned to the kitchen they were giggling.

"Mum, you fancy him, don't you?"

Ria nudged Millie.

"Now then, you two, let's get on with preparing dinner and you can tell me what you've been up to."

Hattie didn't want to share her attraction to Justin with them at the moment.

Chapter 11

Fado

I was terrified in the hospital. I did not like the nurses asking all those questions. I could tell that Hattie was very worried about them asking about my past. I was really scared that someone at the hospital would take me away from Hattie and I clung tightly to her. I was relieved when they said I could go home with a temporary cast on my arm but I was not looking forward to my next visit.

Hattie tried to keep me in the house with my cast on but I just wanted to go to the stables and look after Bubbles. I was sure I could manage with one arm. It was great that Ria and Millie came down to visit us. I was really worried when the man and nurse turned up at the farm. I didn't really understand what they wanted but Justin seemed to sort it out. It was a good job he turned up just at the right time!

Three days after the injury I was out at the yard and everyone made a big fuss of me. I got my cast signed by all the kids at the stables.

The cold weather was setting in and that meant the horses and ponies had to stay in at night. I helped as much as I could on the yard with filling hay nets and water buckets. Hattie became very concerned that there was not enough time to help me learn English. I did want to go to school like the other kids at the stables. I was nervous though and had lots of questions to ask Hattie.

"Who will be in my class, Hattie?"

"Lots of boys and girls your age. You will make new friends."

"But what about my friends at the stables? Will they be in my class?"

"Well, I am not sure who, if anyone from the stables will be in your class, they might be."

"What can I have for my lunch? Some of my friends take their food in lovely lunchboxes, can I have one of my own?"

"OK, love, if you want a packed lunch we will buy you a lunchbox."

I was taken to the school to meet the teachers and have a look round. It was a bit frightening seeing all those children sitting in their classrooms. I wasn't sure how I would cope with having to stay inside for so long each day. I hadn't been able to go to the school in Kenya as I was the oldest son and had to help Mamma with all the chores. I really wanted to make it work though as if I was clever enough. I would be able to get a job and earn enough money to find and help my family.

"Fado will be able to start after half term," the head teacher told Hattie.

She held out her hand for me to shake it. I felt really worried and hid behind Hattie's leg.

"Fado, shake Miss Hogan's hand, please remember your manners!"

Hattie was going red in the face and looking cross.

"I will see you soon." I said shaking her hand a putting on a brave smile.

Hattie took me shopping for the lunchbox and school uniform. At last, the day arrived for me to start school.

"Hattie, I'm going to miss Bubbles," I said on the drive there.

"Don't be silly; days will fly past and you'll see him when you get back."

When we go to the school gates I clung on to Hattie.

"Look, Fado, Josie is over there with Jan and Ellie."

Hattie had spotted a group of girls from the stables.

"Hi, girls."

I dragged Hattie across to them and they were pleased when they all turned around, patted me on the back and welcomed me into the group.

"Would you girls mind be looking after Fado for me?"

"No, of course not, we'll show him where to go when the bell goes," Josie reassured Hattie.

"Bye, Hattie."

I waved Hattie off now that I was feeling confident with my friends.

My first day was quite scary; first of all, the teacher who was called Miss Topping didn't get my name right.

"Faadooo," she called.

There were giggles from the other children. I didn't answer because it didn't sound like my name. The teacher stared at me waiting for a response. Somehow, I found the confidence to repeat my name correctly.

"Sorry, Fado."

"Yes, Miss Topping," I replied.

Everyone stopped giggling and settled down. I found some of the lessons hard to keep up with but I loved P.E. and art. The day flew past and all too soon I was running across the playground into Hattie's arms. I told Hattie everything that had happened at school and said I wanted to go back tomorrow.

When they arrived back at the farm I wanted to run straight out to see Bubbles.

"No, you will come in and have a drink first. You're not going near the stables wearing that uniform."

"OK!" I called back as I rushed upstairs to change.

"Oh, Bubbles, I've missed you so much. Did you miss me?"

I hugged Bubbles who nuzzled into me.

"I will give you a good groom and then we can go for a ride whilst it's still light."

I chatted to Bubbles non-stop. I was so relieved to get out into the fresh air after spending so much time inside all day.

"Well, don't be too long. It gets dark early now."

"I know, Hattie, that's why I didn't want to waste time getting changed and having a chat."

"Err, excuse me, young man! We'll have less of your cheek."

Hattie smiled to herself as she thought of the poor and frightened weak boy that she had rescued now doing so well that he was able to answer her back.

"Hey, titch, how did your first day at school go?" Sheila's daughter Lauren asked Fado.

"Great, I was best at P.E. 'cos I could climb the big rope and no-one else could."

"Wow, that's really clever. I could never climb that rope in P.E."

"I just loved it but I'm afraid I found the literacy lesson very hard."

"Aw, don't worry. I still find that hard now, but you'll get better."

I smiled at Lauren and skipped off to find the tack for Bubbles.

We managed a quick ride around the pony loop before it got dark. I sorted the barn out for the night and then went to find Hattie. I was starving. She was on the phone looking serious. I decided to get back into the house as I was getting chilled and I remembered the teacher had given me some words to learn.

Hattie helped me when she had put the tea on. The next day was OK at school but I was struggling with having to spend so much time indoors. Also, one of the older kids called me a monkey when I was hanging upside down on the climbing frame. I didn't make a big deal of it but my friend told the teacher and the big boy got really told off and was made to apologise to me. After school he tried to trip me up in the corridor. It was the first time I was made to think about the colour of my skin. The school was in a small village with only white children in it so I did stand out. Most of the children were very kind and wanted to be my friend. The big boy and his group of friends kept pointing and giggling at me. I decided to try and ignore them.

"We have to go for your physiotherapy today," Hattie told me when she appeared at the school gate.

"Oh no, do we have to? My arm is fine now."

"I'm afraid we do; your muscles are still weak after the break."

"I just wanted to get home to Bubbles. I had to admit that my arm did sometimes feel a bit floppy."

The exercises the physio gave me really helped. I loved the P.E. lessons and needed a strong arm for the gym.

Hattie told me about her own childhood. She would be up at the crack of dawn and straight after breakfast, she would get on her scooter and go as fast as it would take her up to the farm where the farmer's three children would be waiting for her.

They would spend the day having many adventures across the fields, in the barns or riding the old ponies. I loved to spend the day at the stables or having adventures of my own in the fields. Hattie said the fresh air made me really healthy. I was getting very strong now. I had been weak when Hattie had first found me. One day, I would be a full-grown man and able to find my family. I was very happy in my life with Hattie but always longed to get back to my mamma, brothers and sisters. Justin had managed to find out my mother's name and origin but not where she was living now. When I was old enough I was going to go and find her myself. I kept this plan to myself as I felt it upset Hattie to go on about my family. I was so lucky to have found her. She was very kind and I will never forget what she has done for me.

Another thing I kept from Hattie was how hard I found it being at school. Not just because I was so far behind my peers academically but also there was the language barrier. I could hold my own conversationally very well now, but some of the language in the lessons was beyond my comprehension. The main problem I had was sitting in a hot centrally heated classroom with false lighting hurting my eyes. I would be wriggling around in my seat after about half an hour longing for playtime when I could get outside and run around. Also, the bully boys were making my time in the playground hard. I didn't know how to handle the problem because if I kept telling the teacher they would just get me after school.

"Sit still, Fado, please take your hands away from your eyes, how can you see the whiteboard?" Miss Topping was constantly telling me.

"Have you got ants in your pants?" she would sometimes say causing an eruption of giggles from my classmates.

Now this puzzled me because I remembered having ants in my pants at certain times of the year back in my homeland when they invaded the mud hut. I didn't like to sound rude but wanted to tell Miss Topping that there wouldn't be ants on my classroom chair!

Hattie always asked me lots of questions about my day at school and I would always try to sound positive about it as I didn't want to worry her.

I did become slightly worried when the teacher sent a letter home with all the class which was inviting the parents to come and talk to her about their child's progress. I tried to make excuses, why Hattie would not need to bother going. However, Hattie told me that she used to be a primary school teacher and would never miss an opportunity to go into the school and see my work.

The week leading up to the school visit I tried really hard to sit still and do the very best work I could.

The dreaded day arrived and instead of running out to the playground to meet Hattie at the end of school, Hattie came into the classroom.

"Hello, Mrs Gee, I am so glad you could make it."

"Well, I never missed any of my own children's parents' evenings. Being a teacher myself, I know how important it is to keep up with their progress."

"That's quite right too. Now, Fado loves P.E. and all the outdoor activities and he really excels at them."

"However, his concentration span for academic work has room for improvement."

I wanted the floor to swallow me up and prayed that my teacher wouldn't go on about the ants. Hattie screwed her face up in disapproval of this negative comment.

"I see; well of course, the classroom is rather alien to Fado's origins. At home he loves spending time out on the farm."

"Well, of course, he is very lucky to have such a wonderful place as yours to grow up in and I can say he is very lucky to have you. However, as you know, we have certain standards to achieve and we have to ensure that all the children reach their targets."

"I do know that and if we can have a daily home/school liaison book then I could help Fado with any difficulties he is having."

"That would be very helpful. Fado, would you like to show Hattie your books? I will leave you to it but please don't hesitate to speak to me before you go if you have any questions."

I was proud to show Hattie my artwork and she admired it greatly but did want to see my literacy and numeracy books. I was not so proud of these as I knew that compared to my other classmates, my work was not so good.

Hattie looked at the books with a fixed smile on her face and did not really say much. Soon, the ordeal was over and to my relief, Hattie said they must go as the horses would be waiting for their tea.

That evening when I had gone to bed I heard Hattie talking to Millie on the phone.

"Well, I was not very impressed, I can tell you; I mean, wouldn't you just make sure he was getting some extra help instead of allowing every piece of work to be unfinished?"

I couldn't help a tear from slipping down my face.

"No, she just said he had concentration problems!"

I made a mental note to find out what that long word meant.

"I told her I want a daily report via a home/school liaison book."

I knew that this would mean doing work with Hattie every night which meant less time with my beloved pony.

"Yes, you can have a look next weekend when you come home. Bye, love, speak soon."

I drifted off to sleep with a heavy heart. I didn't think I would ever be as clever at my school work as Hattie wanted me to be but I knew I could make her proud of me with my work with horses.

Chapter 12

Hattie

Hattie sometimes felt dizzy with everything that was going on in her life. She would lie awake at night in turmoil with events going round and round in her mind. She was constantly anxious and worried about Fado. It was a great relief that Justin had managed to find the documents at the embassy which registered his date of birth and full name. Thankfully, Sheila had been able to pass the information on to the hospital and explain the situation. With his official full name and date of birth she was able to register Fado at school. This presented new worries and problems. How was he going to catch up at school? She felt guilty about her own children. Did she spend enough time involving herself in their lives?

Her son was definitely becoming very distant from her life. He had wrapped himself up in his job and his girlfriend. There seemed no place for her. He just kept asking her to go and visit him. With all that was going on at the farm, Hattie knew she couldn't get away enough to visit him. How could she split herself in so many directions?

There was also the tentative issue of the feelings that had aroused in her innermost self over the lawyer Justin. Should she just dismiss them? After all, she hardly had time for a relationship with everything else going on in her life. But that was easier said than done! She seemed to find reasons to seek his advice and he was more than willing to help her. Her inner voice would say, 'What the heck, life's too short, go with your heart.' Her exterior voice would say, 'Pull yourself together, how on earth would you find time for a relationship?' Hattie would toss and turn at night with these thoughts as the wind and rain battered against her open window and the owls hooted wisely around the house, calling her this way and that way with her life changing decisions.

Fado woke Hattie early one morning crying out. "Hattie! Quick, the storm. I'm frightened."

"It's OK, darling, you are safe here."

Hattie cuddled Fado close to her.

"I had a bad dream. I thought I was back on the boat. Hattie, I won't have to go back on that boat, will I?"

Hattie drew him closer.

"No, of course you won't, you will be safe here on the farm now."

Fado recovered in time for school. Hattie was quiet on the way to school with Fado chattering away. She was debating whether to speak to his teacher about her disappointment on seeing his work yesterday. Her daughter Millie had said she should but she didn't want to cause trouble for Fado.

"Now be a good boy, Fado. I really want you to try hard and get your work finished today, please."

"But, Hattie, the teacher never lets me finish. She says I shouldn't have been looking out of the window."

"Well, your teacher is right. Why were you looking out of the window?"

"Cos I can't help watching the squirrels playing, they are so funny and clever. I wish I could be like them, outside all day."

"Fado, you cannot be a squirrel. You are a little boy and you have to work hard at school if you want to get anywhere in life."

I wish I could be clever like the other children, I thought to myself because I really wanted to please Hattie. I told Hattie that I would try but secretly I felt that I could be a great horseman without being clever at school.

Hattie left Fado in the playground and switched her attentions to the busy day ahead at the stables. With the weather so bad it was all hands-on deck to keep the horses fed and exercised. She also needed to find time to talk to Justin.

The day flew past at the stables with endless rounds of mucking out as there was no turnout today so that the horses and ponies could have their legs dry and checked for mud fever. All too soon it was time to collect Fado from school.

To Hattie's delight, he came running out to her with a 'well done' certificate for excellent number work. Hattie picked him up and swung him round. She looked in the home/school liaison book. The teacher said there was a big improvement in his concentration and as a result, he had been able to complete his work.

When Fado had gone to bed and before she sat down and fell asleep, Hattie picked up the phone.

"Justin, it's me Hattie."

"HATTIE! How lovely to hear from you. What can I do for you?"

"Look, it's all too much to explain over the phone, could we meet up?"

Justin took in a deep breath to stem the excitement in his voice.

"Well, of course. Would you like to pop around to mine tomorrow morning?"

"It would have to be after I have done the horses although I haven't got riders in the morning, so it would be around eleven by the time I have finished the jobs."

"Perfect, just in time for coffee then. You have my address, so you can find me, OK?"

"Yes, no problem, the satnav will find the way to you. See you tomorrow."

Hattie had a restless night worrying about waking up early enough to get everything done so that she could get to Justin's house on time. She could barely contain her excitement at the thought of seeing him again. Sheila asked her what was up as she was acting like the cat that had got the cream.

Hattie did not want to tell anyone about her feelings for Justin. She was a bit embarrassed if the truth was known.

"I mean, a woman of my age going all gooey over a chap I barely know. I can hardly admit it to myself, never mind anyone else."

She made excuses to Sheila about needing to go shopping at 10:30 a.m. as she rushed inside to wash and change, not forgetting a spray of perfume to get rid of any lingering horsey smells. As an afterthought she found some lipstick in her handbag and slapped some on to brighten up her pale winter face.

Following the satnav instructions, she was soon at Justin's front door. As if he had been looking out for her, he opened the door whilst she still had her hand in the air after knocking.

Their eyes locked for an intense moment and it was all Hattie could do to pull herself together.

"Hi there, well, are you going to invite me in? That coffee smells good."

"Of course, come in, sorry, it's just lovely to see you again. You look really well If I might say so."

"Do I? Well, I don't always feel it at this time of year with all the hard work, worn out more like!"

"Come and sit down and I will get you some shortcake and a nice hot coffee. I really don't know how you can cope outside with this harsh winter."

Hattie really appreciated the coffee and biscuits.

"I just need to know if I can get help with making Fado more secure in this country. Does it mean that he can stay here now that I'm his legal guardian?"

"Well, there's no certainty. I mean, if his mother were to get in touch with the embassy, he'd probably go back to Kenya."

"Of course, I accept that; it's just that, the incident at the hospital unnerved me."

Hattie put her head in her hands. Justin went over to her putting his arms around her.

"Listen, my love, you are a wonderful person who has given Fado a happy, secure and loving home. No one is going to take him away from you."

The warm and sympathetic voice was all too much for Hattie and she broke down. Justin rocked her in his arms until she recovered.

"You've got so much on your plate, Hattie, it's bound to take its toll; good to have a cry sometimes."

Justin was so kind. Hattie composed herself.

"I'm sorry, Justin, it's just that I've grown so very fond of the boy."

"Well, stop worrying so much about what might never happen and just carry on with the good work of caring for him."

Hattie felt much better although she was a bit embarrassed about breaking down in front of Justin.

She was contemplating this when he surprised her with his next comment.

"Hattie, I would very much like to take you out to dinner."

Hattie's heart began to beat very fast. This had come out of the blue. She had no idea that Justin felt the same way about her as she did about him.

"Oh, well, you do surprise me, err I'm not sure…"

"Of course, no you are far too busy, I expect you are chock-a-block in the evenings; sorry, I should have been more thoughtful. Perhaps, you and Fado could make a Sunday lunch?"

Justin tried to hide the disappointment in his voice but he felt devastated. It was obvious that Hattie did not feel the same way for him as he for her.

"No, it's not that at all, I could get Sheila to babysit one evening. I would love to join you for dinner."

"Excellent, would Friday night suit you? I'll pick you up at seven?"

"7:30 p.m. would be better as we have Pony Club on Fridays."

"Great, see you Friday then."

Hattie couldn't help smiling to herself all the way home. She put on her Celine Dion CD and sang along at the top of her voice.

When Hattie arrived back at the yard she had no time to think about her meeting with Justin as the master of the hunt was talking to Sheila.

"Ah, there you are; I was just telling the master that I was not sure where you had gone or what time you would be back."

"Well, I am back now, what can I do for you, Master?"

"Top of the morning to you, Hattie. We were wondering how you'd be fixed for the meeting here on Tuesday the 20th?"

"Oh my, I expect we could manage that, couldn't we, Sheila?"

"We would have to keep those horses and ponies not going in, but that won't be a problem this time of year."

"Brilliant, can you manage the hunt staff parking here, Hattie?" the master addressed them both.

Hattie answered.

"Yes, yourself, of course, Master."

"Great see you on the 20th."

Hattie and Sheila waved the master off, then turned to each other and said at the same time, "Wow, that's exciting."

Sheila told Hattie that she thought the Hunt must have a very high opinion of her to have asked her to hold a meeting. Hattie said there was much to be done to make the place presentable for the meeting.

Hattie was excited about the meeting and set about ringing a few friends to help out with the food. She was so preoccupied with the arrangements that she completely forgot about her date with Justin.

Chapter 13

Justin

Justin had thought about nothing else since the meeting with Hattie. Every time he saw her, his heart grew fonder of her. He surprised himself at his patience. He was used to instant results once he set his mind to something, but with Hattie, he realised that rushing into things would just drive her away. She had such a strong and independent character. The relationship had to develop at her pace if it was going to at all. His role was just to suggest things incidentally and hope that she agreed.

He realised that Hattie was not the type of person to do anything she didn't want to and her life already seemed very full; he worried there would be no room for him to enter into it. Having turned all this around in his head during the sleepless nights he was having since meeting Hattie, he felt that accepting his invitation to dinner was a real breakthrough. However, he was nervous that the conversation would turn to his past and he would have to be quick off the mark to change the subject. Before the date, he had to find out something about the boys' origins which meant another call to Tristan.

"Good morning, Tristan, how are you?"

"Hello, there my good fellow, long time no see. I thought we were going to have a drink for old times' sake!"

"Yes we were. Sorry, old chap, the days just fly by as work has really taken off now."

"Not to worry. How about Friday night? I could meet you at the Conservative Club. I have connections with it and would welcome a weekend down your way catching up with old friends."

Oh, Lord, that's all I need, a clash with Tristan and Hattie, how am I going to get out of this? Justin had to find a quick excuse for Tristan.

"Ah, that would be tricky this Friday. I have a meeting with a client; how about one evening next week?"

"Mmm, meeting clients on a Friday night? Sounds pretty serious to me. OK, I'll stay over and meet you on Monday. Now what was the purpose of your call?"

"Oh yes, Monday's fine. It was about the servant boy again. Social services are trying to find out his date of birth and full name. Did you have any records of your servants?"

"Good Lord, that's a tall order. Even if I did have any records (which I didn't), they would have been lost in the shipwreck. If you got onto the embassy in Nairobi they may be able to help as the servants were supposed to register births and deaths."

"OK, thanks, I'll get onto them. See you on Monday then."

Justin put the phone down wondering how he was going to get out of Monday night. The last thing he wanted was for Hattie to think that he was socialising with Tristan.

Justin found out the number of the embassy and dialled it. He realised it was a long shot as he didn't have a great deal of information to give them about Fado. To his surprise, they did not dismiss his request and said they would ring him back when they had found out the information. Justin was so excited at this unexpected response that he could not wait to tell Hattie. He picked up the phone, but soon wished he hadn't.

Chapter 14

Hattie

The hunt meeting to be held at her farm was taking up lots of time with the preparations. Hattie was quite flattered to have been asked to host it and wanted everyone to really enjoy themselves. It was difficult to get enough volunteers to help as it was a week day. She admitted she could have done it with a man at her side to organise it and she thought of asking Justin. However, things were not good there either.

She had been putting off calling him. She was going to have to cancel Friday night's dinner date. With all that was going on, she had completely forgotten it was the hunt race night and she had been asked to do the tote. Poor Hattie was suffering from bad stomach cramps in the mornings and knew it was anxiety.

Fado was also testing her patience as all he wanted to do was to be out at the stables playing with the ponies. His school work was way below standard for his age and the teachers were on her back all the time to help him more at home. All he was on about at the moment was having the day off for the hunt meeting. Hattie knew she would feel proud to see him all dressed up on Bubbles at the meeting. Sheila who had grown very fond of the boy, wanted to be part of it all by looking after him.

However, the teachers certainly would not approve of him missing school for the hunt and she suspected Miss Topping was an anti by the disapproving looks she got when she had gone to pick up Fado in her hunting outfit on Tuesdays.

The worst thing was that there was too much on her mind and no time to deal with it. There were several problems at the stables with the horses. It had been a terrible and wet winter and the turnout fields were horribly muddy. Some horses and ponies were getting mud fever and had to be kept in and some were getting other problems like cellulites from standing in too much. Luckily these were mostly the livery horses but even so, Hattie had never known so many vets coming and going to her yard. Hattie was deep in thought and warming her hands around her coffee cup when the phone rang.

"Hello, Hattie, how are you doing?"

"Oh, hi, Justin, I was going to ring you."

"Well, I have saved you a call and have good news. I couldn't wait until tomorrow night to tell you."

"Oh, Lord, is it Thursday already? I should have rung you before."

"No, don't apologise, you are a very busy lady. I am ringing to tell you that the embassy in Nairobi sent through all of Fado's papers now including his birth certificate. We'll be able to give copies to the school and social workers."

"That is brilliant news. That will get social services off my back. Well done, Justin, I can't thank you enough for this."

"It's a pleasure and you can buy me a drink tomorrow night, if you like?"

"Ah, about tomorrow night, I am terribly sorry I didn't ring you before but I can't make it."

"Oh no, why not?"

"Well, it's the hunt race night and I have to do the tote. I tell you what, why don't you come along? It will be a fun evening."

Hattie felt guilty at how disappointed Justin sounded when she told him she couldn't meet him. She had no idea how he would get on with her hunting friends.

"Err, I am disappointed about our dinner date but OK, I will only come along if I can give you a lift. Pick you up at seven?"

"Great, I look forward to seeing you and catching up."

Justin put the phone down and let out a long despairing sigh.

"Am I ever going to get close to that lady? I can't imagine her having time for me. Should I just give up now or soldier on in the hope that one day…"

Hattie put down the phone feeling terrible. Life as usual was moving on at a great speed with so many things to deal with day to day. It was a real juggling act. *Well, that has sort of killed two birds with one stone,* thought Hattie. I can help the hunt and see Justin although I won't be devoting all my attention to him as I am doing the tote. Hattie told herself off for involving him in a hunt do where he wouldn't even know anyone. She considered ringing him back and scrapping the arrangement. *Well at least, I'll get to see him on the way there and back. It would be nice to get a lift then I can enjoy a glass of wine without worrying about driving.*

Hattie had not had time to think about Justin lately and she thought her crush on him was fading. Besides, there was no time in her life for relationships and all the complications and problems they bring with them.

"I know it's a struggle on my own sometimes but I have my wonderful children and it's better I stay that way for all those concerned." Hattie told herself to keep her distance from Justin on Friday night.

Justin went out to the 'Farmers Friend' and bought a tweed jacket and tie with foxes on it. He wanted to impress Hattie but feared she thought of him as a real town boy. If he looked the part she might be drawn closer to him. He was a little nervous about going to a hunt do with her. That was her world and she would be surrounded by like-minded people who respected her. He wouldn't know anyone unless there were some farmer clients of his there, but he was determined to socialise and enjoy the evening for Hattie's sake.

Friday night came all too soon for Hattie, she hadn't had time to think about what she was going to wear and needed to wash her hair. It had been such a busy week but luckily one of the stable girls was free to babysit Fado. He had pleaded with her to go to the race night saying that he wanted to be a jockey when he grew up and needed to go and watch how they rode. Hattie had to laugh. He would probably make a good little jockey. But she was not letting him go. It would be difficult to keep an eye on him when she was doing the tote. Then, there was the added complication of Justin and she had no intention of getting Fado involved with him.

Hattie dashed in from the stables with half an hour to get herself ready. She left Fado eating beans on toast in front of the telly feeling guilty as this was something she would never normally have agreed to him doing.

By the time she had got downstairs, Holly was sitting next to Fado with a bowl of Maltesers and they waved a quick goodbye as she flew out of the door. Hattie wanted to wait in the porch for Justin rather than Fado answering the door to him. Justin was pulling up outside as she closed the front door.

Hattie had to catch her breath as his lovely smile lit up his face at the sight of her.

"Hello, how are you?" Justin was saying as he jumped out of the car to open the door for her.

"Oh well, it was a bit of a rush to get ready this early, sorry my hair is a bit wet."

Hattie suddenly felt herself blush as she realised that she hadn't really glanced in the mirror to check what she looked like. She thought Justin looked very dapper in his tweed jacket and checked shirt with fox tie.

She had only ever seen him in casual clothes and her heart skipped a beat at how handsome he looked.

"My dear, you look lovely, scrubbed up very well, you have."

Justin felt an embarrassing stirring in between his legs as Hattie got into the car showing him her beautiful long legs as she did so.

Hattie directed him to the village hall talking all the time about the hunt and its characters. By the time they got there Justin felt he knew some of the main members that he would be meeting.

As soon as they entered the hall Hattie was greeted with a stream of people shouting, 'Hi Hattie,' and people beckoning her over to them. To his surprise, Hattie linked arms with Justin and took him over to her friends.

"Hi, this is Justin, the lawyer helping me with Fado's case."

This was a good move as it seemed Fado was very popular with all who met him and they beamed at Justin and told him that it was great he was helping Hattie to find out about his origins. Some people said that Hattie had told them all about him.

All too soon Hattie was whisked away to do the tote. Justin was invited to join the master's table and he realised he was on a show here. He didn't know the first thing about hunting and he couldn't even ride a horse so he was feeling a little out of his comfort zone. Luckily, he had the gift of the gab and was able to blag it.

After everyone had downed a few pints they didn't seem to worry about his lack of knowledge and when the races got going he was as excited as anyone about his horse winning.

Hattie was worried about Justin. She hadn't meant for him to sit on the master's table and hoped he wouldn't show himself up with his lack of knowledge in both the hunting and the equine world. Every time she glanced over at his table he seemed to be having a great time even though he was only on the orange juice whereas the rest of the guests were downing pints like there was no tomorrow. With the first race over Hattie jumped up and went over to him. Justin jumped up and offered to buy her a drink. They went to the bar and Hattie asked him if he was OK. Justin assured her he was having a great time with the best company. He told Hattie he had been asked if he was taking her to the ball. Hattie was surprised that her friends had been so presumptuous to think that he would be her escort for the ball.

"Oh, the ball, well if you would like to go, I can always add you on to our table."

"Sounds great and I will buy the tickets for us tonight, Libby on our table is selling them."

"Are you sure, Justin? They are quite expensive."

"Of course, look here she comes. Libby, can we have two tickets for the ball please?"

Libby winked and nodded at Hattie as she took the tickets out. Hattie felt herself going red and after thanking Libby, she made her excuses to get back to the tote. She was taken aback about how fast things were moving with Justin. She hadn't expected him to fit in so well with her hunting crowd. He had also offered to help her at the meeting saying that he could easily rearrange his clients for the day so that he would be free to hand out the port and whisky.

Hattie was trying to get her head round to sorting the tickets out for the next race when she heard a shout from across the room.

"Justin, my old friend, what the heck are you doing here?"

A crowd had burst through the door, some with red coats on, all with red faces obviously rolled in from the local pub.

The loud man who had shouted across the room had now got Justin in a bear hug. Hattie was taken aback that someone knew Justin so well. She recognised the red coat as the master from the visiting hunt they had hosted that week. When Justin had finally been released she could see the loud man's face. To her horror, she recognised him; it was the horrible Tristan from her horseback safari in Kenya. The one who had Fado's family as servants! She couldn't believe her eyes! What was he doing here? Worse than that, how did he know Justin so well!

Chapter 15

Fado

I was really fond of Sheila; she was so patient and caring to me at the stables. Whenever   I needed help she dropped what she was doing for me.

"Sheila, can you tell Hattie that I have to be at the meeting on Tuesday, PLEASE?"

"Fado, no one can tell Hattie anything, least of all me."

"I know, but you are the only person who may be able to persuade her. We need to tell her that it's for Bubbles' sake. I have to be there on him."

******

Sheila adored the boy and would do anything to help him. She admired Hattie in everything she had achieved at the stables. Building up a successful business from nothing and although her work load was very hard, she would do all she could to help and support her. Hattie was a unique person and Sheila aspired to be like her. It was amazing how the little waif had come her way, an unbelievable story, but then that was Hattie, things happened to her that no one else would believe.

"OK, Fado, I will see what I can do, I am on your side and do want you to go to the meeting."

"Oh thanks, I know you can persuade Hattie. I am going to clean my tack. It needs lots of oiling before the hunt."

Sheila had to smile as Fado skipped off. *That boy will go far in the horse world,* she thought to herself. Sheila didn't know how she was going to persuade Hattie to let him go to the meeting. She did really want to take him and would be proud to show everyone what a good rider he was now. She felt she had contributed to his progress.

******

I love being responsible for Bubbles, all his care and am glad that not many other people ride him at the moment. I don't like it when they do. I stand at the arena and watch to make sure the rider isn't pulling Bubbles in the mouth. I took the saddle and bridle out of the locker and went to the shed to find the oil and Hattie's own tack cleaner. I didn't want to just use the same spray as all the others used as this was a special occasion. I found the leather balm, cleaned all the tack with that and then I went to find the oil. I couldn't see it anywhere at first but then I spotted a large container on the floor under the shelf. It was very heavy. I looked around the yard to see if there was anyone who could help me. Everyone was busy working so I took the top off and dipped the cloth into the container. This didn't work as the oil was too far down the container. I took hold of the handle and tipped the container onto the cloth. This turned out to be a disaster as the container was far too heavy for me to lift. My hand slipped and the container fell over spilling the oil all over the floor.

On hearing the crash, the dogs ran into the shed and began lapping up the oil. I knew this would make them sick; shouting and trying to push them out of the shed, I skidded on the oil and fell out of the shed door. I caught my ankle and it was bleeding through my boots. The dogs left the oil and jumped all over me licking my face.

"What on earth is going on here?" exclaimed Sheila as she ran up the yard and helped Fado up.

The dogs left Fado and went back to licking the oil.

"Oh, my Lord, what is the oil doing all over the floor?"

I was crying by this time; my ankle was really hurting.

"You know, you shouldn't be in this shed at all, Fado, never mind meddling with the oil!"

"I know, but I wanted my tack to look really good for the hunt. Oh, Sheila, please help me clean it up before Hattie sees it or she will never let me go to the hunt."

"Go and fetch me the blue paper roll from the tea room and we will see if we can mop up this mess."

The dogs followed me as I hobbled to the tea room.

"I had better start with mopping you up. Take your boot off and let's see the damage."

I was very grateful for Sheila's help as she cleaned my cut ankle. I helped her mop up the rest of the oil which soaked into the blue kitchen roll.

"Thanks, Sheila, can you get me a bit of oil to do my tack with now please?"

"Yes I can, but please do not touch that oil container again."

"I won't; do you think the dogs will be sick after licking it?"

"Well, they will be out here for a couple of hours yet so if they are it won't be so bad. Hattie won't be back for a while, let's hope they are all OK by then."

I finished my tack and put it back in the locker. My ankle was still stinging a bit but it had stopped bleeding.

By the time Hattie came out to the yard to find me all was back to normal. I was relieved to have got away with that little disaster. I adored Hattie and knew she was a bit stressed at the moment as it was a hard time of the year with all the work at the stables, so I wouldn't want to give her more trouble.

Unfortunately, I had forgotten about the dogs. When they were having their dinner, they began to throw up and later that evening, they had problems at the other end making the house stink. I just pretended I didn't know why they had such bad tummies!

The next day with all the dog mess cleaned up and the house smelling of disinfectant, Hattie was not in a very good mood taking me to school. I decided to try really hard today to get a merit so that I could cheer her up. I thought it best not to bring up the subject of going to the hunt meeting and the best way to get around her was by working really hard at school for the rest of the week. If I collect lots of merit cards I am sure Hattie won't be able to say I can't go to the meeting. I really struggled with reading and writing and found it very difficult to keep up in class.

After school I ran into Hattie's arms in the school playground with two merits, one for maths and one for my science project.

Chapter 16

Hattie

"Whatever is going on? I cannot believe that, Tristan, the horrid, racist, pompous and unpleasant man from our horseback safari in Kenya has turned up at one of our hunt social events! And what is he doing giving Justin a bear hug?" Hattie was talking to herself.

"Hattie, are you with us? The tote is open for the next race and here come the crowds. You are on numbers five, six and seven."

Jo jolted Hattie back into the job she was here to do. She would have to put what she had just witnessed behind her and get on with it. It was at times like this that she was grateful for her past experience in amateur dramatics as she had the ability to put on an act.

She laughed and joked along as the people placed their bets telling her why they had chosen the horse they were betting on.

As soon as the lights went out as the next race was starting, she felt a tap on her shoulder. It was Justin.

"Come outside for a minute," he whispered in her ear sending shivers down her neck.

She got up and followed him, eager to hear his explanation.

Things had got rather committed this evening with him buying her tickets for the ball and she had asked him to help her with her meeting on Tuesday.

"Hattie, you must be wondering what on earth my connection with Tristan is? I can explain everything."

"Well, I hope you can, I was quite shocked to see how friendly he was with you after all we have said about him!"

"That is just what he is like, making out he is everyone's best friend. I did know him when I was in Kenya, we were at the same expats club."

"Then why didn't you tell me this before?"

"I know I should have, but look, Hattie, the truth is..."

"Justin, I have to get back inside, so come on, I need an explanation quickly, because you should know me by now, I only deal with honest people."

"The honest truth is, I am very fond of you and I didn't tell you about my connection with Tristan because I was afraid that you wouldn't have anything more to do with me if I told you."

"Well, you had better tell me now because before we go any further I will not have any secrets between us."

Hattie could feel herself getting hot and red faced. She was so upset that she may have misjudged Justin. She thought him as kind, caring and sensitive, but if he had been a friend of Tristan's he could not be genuine. Embarrassingly, she felt tears prick the back of her eyes and she had to get away from Justin before he could see how upset she was.

"Well, I have got to get back to the tote," Hattie managed to say as she rushed back inside hearing Justin shout after her,

"No wait, Hattie, let me explain."

Justin was beside himself with disappointment and frustration. Things had been going so well and now they were so terribly bad. How was he going to repair the damage Tristan had done with his over-the-top greeting? He didn't feel he could go back into the room so he just stood outside the toilets waiting for the event to finish and hoping he could explain to Hattie about Tristan on the way home, that is, if she would accept a lift from him. He knew what she said about being truthful and he felt the same but he didn't think he could ever tell her about his real connection with Tristan. He spent the next hour in turmoil going over and over what he would say to Hattie. He could not lose her now.

"Hey, Hattie, where's your friend got to? You kept him quiet, didn't you? Don't blame you, he is rather dishy."

"Oh, Daisy, have you got the hots for him? He, err, had to go early, some business to deal with." Hattie tried to sound light hearted when she felt quite the opposite.

She would have to try and get a lift home from someone if Justin had left. Poor Hattie found it hard to focus on the tote whilst looking at the door to see if Justin was coming back through it. Also, she could hear Tristan's loud hearty laugh with his rowdy friends. This sent shivers up her spine and she couldn't help turning her mouth up as she was filled with unpleasant memories of him. It was a great relief when the last race was over and she could make a dash for the toilet and car park to see if Justin had left. If he had she would go back inside and see who was going her way to give her a lift home. Although she thought it would be unreasonable of him to have left without her.

"Hattie, here I am, are you ready to go?"

Hattie jumped as Justin appeared outside the toilets.

"Well, I am not sure I should accept a lift home with you, I was just going to go back in and find someone else."

"Oh no, please don't do that, I need to explain about Tristan to you."

Justin was anxious to get Hattie away before Tristan came out and was all over him again. He put his hand in the rear of her back and guided her towards the car. To his relief, she didn't object too much. Hattie reluctantly got into the front seat beside Justin. Her face as usual said it all, she was upset.

"I can appreciate how upsetting it was for you seeing Tristan."

"Well, it was more of a shock seeing him at a hunt meeting. What was upsetting was seeing him being so matey with you!"

"I know but he was an acquaintance from the past. I never expected to see him either; maybe he was so friendly because I had been in contact with him about Fado."

Hattie had to admit that Justin's contact with Tristan had been very helpful in finding out about Fado's origins. Maybe she was overreacting. She turned to look at Justin. He was gripping the steering wheel and his face was contorted with anxiety. Hattie couldn't help feeling sorry for him.

"Look, Justin, I am really grateful for all you have done in finding out about Fado and I do understand that it meant you had to get in touch with Tristan to do that."

Justin relaxed his grip on the steering wheel and turned to Hattie.

"Oh, Hattie, I would do anything to help you. The truth is I have grown so very fond of you."

Before he could stop himself he leant over and began kissing Hattie passionately on the lips. To his surprise she didn't resist and this encouraged him to get into a very deep embrace. Nothing else mattered, he lost all sense of his surroundings, such was the joy and ecstasy of this longed-for moment.

It was Hattie who pulled away first, breathless and hot after the most intimate of kisses she had experienced for a very long time with this very handsome man whom she had not even dared to admit her feelings for before now.

"Oh, Justin, that was lovely, but I think we had better get moving before we get towed off the field!"

"Hattie, you have no idea how long I have wanted to kiss you like that, thank you so much. You are right, we are the last to leave."

Hattie put the Tristan thing to the back of her mind as she got herself to bed that night, falling straight to sleep with butterflies in her stomach.

Chapter 17
Fado

I loved Saturdays. I felt really important as the working girls and boys would always ask me to help them with their jobs whilst they had to lead the ponies around in the lessons. I filled hay nets although I still could not tie them up as they were too heavy for me. I skipped out the pony barn, being careful not to leave any poo behind, although I sometimes needed help wheeling the barrow up the ramp if it was too full. Best of all, I liked grooming the horses and ponies ready for their lesson. Today there was excitement amongst the girls and boys about Tuesday's meeting. They had been allowed to take the day off school. One girl's head mistress had even given permission as they were doing a project on countryside pursuits. The others had said they had dentist or doctors' appointments.

Hattie had still not agreed for me to have the day off. I had concocted a plan with Sheila. She was going to collect me from school saying I had a dentist appointment and take me back after the meeting. I was happy with this as I knew Bubbles would not be able to do the whole hunt. Sheila had promised to lead me across the first field with the huntsman and the hounds. Hattie had promised I could do the same at the children's meeting at half term.

I was a bit worried about Hattie as she seemed distant and a bit dreamy. On Monday night when she was tucking me in at bedtime, I asked her if he could go to the meeting if Sheila collected him from school and took me back afterwards. To my surprise she said that she thought that a very good idea. I put this sudden change in her decision down to her new mood.

I was up at the crack of dawn to get Bubbles ready before I went to school. Hattie was also up very early preparing the food for the meeting before she went to the stables. She dropped me at the school gate with a note for the teacher about the dental appointment.

"You can't really afford to miss an English lesson. Couldn't you have gone to the dentist after school?"

Miss Topping was not very happy about me going anywhere when it was English lessons.

"You will have to have extra homework tonight to make up for what you miss."

"OK, Miss Topping, I will do the work at home."

I couldn't help smiling with excitement about the hunt. I quickly turned away from the teacher so she wouldn't see.

By the time Sheila had picked me up and they were back at the stables, all the horses were plaited up and ready for the hunt and the girls had even done a running Arab plait on Bubbles' long mane. Everyone looked so smart in their tweed jackets.

"Oh, Hattie, you look really smart."

I was very impressed with Hattie in her shiny black boots and smart black jacket with the crisp white stock underneath. The sun was coming out making the horses coats gleam.

"I am so happy to be here!" I shouted out to everyone.

"Come on now, lad, we should be getting ourselves round to the house before the huntsman and hounds arrive."

Sheila took me down to the house on the lead rein. Soon the huntsman and the hounds arrived and the helpers began handing out the sandwiches, roast potatoes and port. Everyone was chatting, eating and drinking. I counted twenty-five horses and riders which the master said was a record for a Tuesday. Sheila took me and Bubbles to stand next to the huntsman with his beautiful bright bay horse. The hounds were standing behind him as good as gold.

"Here, Granite. Come back, Whisky."

The whip kept calling out their names if they began to wander off. He was called that because he had a stick with a long piece of leather on the end to keep the hounds in order.

"I can't believe you know them all by their names, there are so many," I called up to the whip on his beautiful dark bay horse.

"There are ten couple, you can help keep an eye out for me so that we don't lose any."

"What do you mean ten couple?"

"They are all counted in couples."

"Oh, I see, so they all have a buddy, our school does that. The older kids have a buddy with a younger kid."

"Well, that's the same as the hounds; an older one helps a younger one."

I thought this was a great idea. Bubbles seemed to like them and wanted to get nearer to them, Sheila had a job to hold onto me. Suddenly, Grackle, a large tri-coloured hound, ran up to Bubbles and hid behind him before the whipper-in could crack his whip at him; everyone laughed and a few of the foot followers were quick enough to get a photo of us.

After about half an hour, the master stood up in his stirrups, took his hat off and gave a speech. He had to shout as the hounds all began to get excited and bark. When the speech was over the huntsman blew his horn and they were off. Sheila could hardly keep up with Bubbles as he trotted down the farm drive and into the field, trying to keep up with everyone.

"Fado, we can't go into the field with them because I will never be able to hold onto you."

"I am OK, Sheila, I can go by myself."

Hattie had given Sheila strict instructions not to let go of Bubbles. They got to the field entrance and all the horses and hounds were trotting in through the gate. Suddenly, Bubbles reared up and launched himself forward; the gateway was muddy and Sheila slipped over, letting go of Bubbles. I managed to grab the lead rope and threw it over his neck before they were off galloping up the field trying to catch up with the master. A few people tried to lean down and catch hold of the rope, but Bubbles was going too fast for them. I was a bit worried about how he was going to stop but I loved every minute of it. Bubbles caught up with Crystal and then he started to slow down as he felt safe with this matriarch mare. Hattie was very surprised to see him running beside her.

"Are you OK, Fado, where is Sheila?"

"She fell over in the gateway but I love this!"

"Oh no, poor Sheila, stay with me and we will stop at the hunting gate."

Hattie was on Crystal and was relieved that Bubbles had steadied up.

By the time they got to the hunting gate, which would lead them out onto the common, Bubbles was following the hounds and gathering speed.

Hattie could see Sheila running up the field.

"You will have to go back with Sheila now, as that's enough galloping around for poor Bubbles."

"Fado, pull on the reins," called Hattie.

"I can't!" I shouted as I clung on to the front of the saddle.

Bubbles saw a gap in the hedge and pushed his way through just as I had done when I fell down the badger set where Hattie found me. I was scared that Bubbles would fall down one as well. Bubbles squeezed through the hedge and was dodging the trees in pursuit of the hounds. Suddenly, he stopped dead at a fox hole and put his head down snorting. I jumped off him trying to pull his head up. The whipper caught up with us, he was on foot and I wondered what he had done with his horse.

"Come on, you two, let's get you out of here."

He lifted me up and led Bubbles back to the hunting gate where Sheila and Hattie were waiting.

"Oh, thank goodness, you're OK."

Sheila looked as if she was crying.

"I'm so sorry, I couldn't hold on to you," she said.

"Don't be silly, Sheila, you could not have hung onto him and there's no harm done apart from you being covered in mud," Hattie reassured Sheila.

I was surprised that she wasn't really cross with me for not being able to stop Bubbles.

"Now, young man," Hattie was off Crystal with her arm round me, "You've been lucky this time. But I hope you've learnt your lesson now!"

Sheila led Bubbles and me back down the field whilst the rest of the hunt went through the gate and onto the common.

After I had sponged Bubbles down I got changed back into my school uniform and Sheila took me back to school.

"This has been the best day of my life, Sheila. I want to be a huntsman when I grow up."

Sheila had to laugh as she thought of the spectacle of little Bubbles galloping along with all the big horses not much bigger than one of the hounds.

"Fado, I think you can be whatever type of horseman you want when you grow up."

Chapter 18

Justin

Justin found it hard to concentrate on his cases at work after the race night. He could barely sleep for dreaming of Hattie and had to pinch himself as he couldn't believe that wonderful kiss. Had he really managed to get so intimate with this strong, amazing character? Especially after that crazy Tristan had nearly blown it for him. He wondered whether to ring Tristan and tell him not to be so gushing the next time he saw him if he was with Hattie. No, that would be really difficult; best to just try and avoid seeing him.

Justin could hardly wait for the day of the meeting when he would see Hattie again. He had tried to ring her, but she never seemed to answer her phone. She had texted him though.

"Thanks for offering to help at the meeting on Tuesday. Can you get to mine at ten and will you be OK serving the port?"

Justin was slightly disappointed that there was no mention of Friday night or the kiss. But he had replied and said that he would be there and that he was looking forward to seeing her again. She had replied with, 'Me too, x.' Justin realised that he would have to be happy with that until Tuesday.

Justin was up at the crack of dawn on the 'big day', he had drunk umpteen cups of tea by eight o'clock. At last, it was time for him to go to Hattie's. Well, he would be a little early but he just couldn't hang around any longer. When he got to the house the door was open and there were several ladies buzzing around the kitchen preparing sandwiches, cutting slices of cake and cooking roast potatoes.

"Hi, I'm Justin."

The ladies all stopped what they were doing to look him up and down.

"Hello, I'm Gill, have you come to help?"

"Yes, Hattie has asked me to help with the port."

Suddenly, the dogs rushed in followed by Hattie and everyone got to work protecting the food from the scavenging dogs who were wagging their tails enthusiastically and nearly knocking everything flying.

"Hi everyone, how's it going? Oh hello, Justin, let me direct you to the port. It's in the other room."

Justin followed Hattie and it hadn't gone unnoticed that her face had flushed when she had seen him!

They were in the dining room at the other side of the house.

"How are you?" Justin managed to say as his heart skipped a beat.

Hattie looked amazing in her black jacket and shiny black boots.

"All the better for seeing you," she replied.

Before they could stop themselves they were in a passionate embrace and it might have gone on and on if Hattie hadn't heard Fado calling.

"I'll have to dash!" she exclaimed as she broke away from Justin.

"There's the port and plastic cups."

Justin didn't know how Hattie could compose herself so quickly but he realised he would have to do the same if he was to be of any help.

Chapter 19

Hattie

Hattie's heart melted when she saw Fado looking so handsome in his tweed jacket with a huge smile on his face and Bubbles' coat was gleaming. Hattie would never have relented and let him have the time off school if her mind had not been so distracted by Justin.

Hattie dashed off to get on her horse feeling that she had been a bit soft and blamed Justin for making her go all soppy. She had a smile on her face as she greeted her horse Crystal but reassured her that she would not have to take second place in her heart. Crystal was the matriarch of the herd and Hattie had trained her from day one during her contact with humans, they had huge respect for each other and Crystal loved to go hunting.

Hattie told all the kids to follow her around to the house where they would wait for the master and the huntsman with his hounds. She was very proud of the immaculately dressed girls with their shining plaited ponies and told them so putting a smile on all their faces. She wished that her own girls were here to be part of it all but she would have to wait until next weekend when they were visiting to show them the photos.

Hattie was surprised to see that a lot of people were arriving as Tuesdays were usually quiet. She counted twenty-five riders in all. The ladies were working hard to get around to everyone with the delicious food. Even Susie had managed to take a bit of time out to help. She really wanted to see Fado joining in and didn't mind handing around the sausages. Justin had found himself a helper as it was difficult to pour the port and hold the cups. Jo was one of Hattie's adult riders. She could see that Justin was a little nervous of going too near the horses.

"Here you are, Hattie, I'm sure you could do with a glass of port. You've had a busy morning."

Jo patted Crystal as Justin handed Hattie the port. She couldn't help noticing Justin's hand lingering on Hattie as he winked at her. Hattie smiled as she blushed and took a large gulp of her port.

Suddenly, Crystal shook and tossed her head around, knocking poor Justin flying. The port fell to the floor with him and when he got up his white shirt was red making him look like a bloodstained warrior.

"Oh no, what a waste of port!" exclaimed Jo.

Hattie could not stop laughing, especially when Steve, the master shouted across that Crystal must be jealous! Poor Justin scuttled off into the house where the ladies wiped him down and he came back out just in time to see the huntsman blow his horn and the riders trotting off after him.

Hattie gave Justin a reassuring wave and then held back to see that Fado was OK. He had been standing right next to the hounds not looking much bigger than them on the little Shetland. He was laughing as Bubbles was jumping around waiting to follow the other riders. Crystal was impatient to get back to the front which she considered her place to be so Hattie gave a 'thumbs up' sign to Sheila who could only nod in reply and let Crystal get up front.

They trotted up the drive and into the open field. Hattie didn't have time to look around and see if everyone was OK before Crystal galloped off up the field. When they got up to the hunting gate at the top, she was able to stop and look down at the others galloping up the field. To her horror, there was Fado on Bubbles coming up the hill as fast as his little legs would carry him, with no sign of Sheila. She stopped at the hunting gate with the rest of the hunt and felt helpless as she watched Bubbles and Fado squeeze through the hedge.

"It's OK, Hattie, the whip's got him!" George shouted from the other side of the gate.

"Oh, thank goodness," Hattie called back.

When she had seen Sheila lead Fado and Bubbles successfully down the hill, she managed to enjoy the rest of the day particularly when everyone told her how much they had enjoyed the meeting.

Chapter 20
Justin

Justin was embarrassed about the port incident but soon got over it when he met Hattie the next day. Typically, she had moved on and made light of the accident, blaming her jealous horse and they ended up falling about laughing. If anything, the whole humiliating affair had endeared her towards him.

They began phoning each other every evening, relating the day's events and discussing any problems they had with their respective lives.

Justin was ecstatic about the way the relationship was progressing.

However, he had the niggling worry about his past and imagined that if Hattie found out about it the relationship would end. They discovered that they had a mutual affinity with the spiritual world.

Justin had also had many encounters with spirits and like Hattie, rarely shared them with anyone as he feared people would think him odd. He had studied Buddhism since leaving Africa and really respected their beliefs. Hattie also felt she had an affinity with their lifestyles. She certainly gave off an air of calm and tranquillity to all around her whether human or animal. He felt they had a great rapport if only he didn't have to deal with his sordid past. He decided to keep it from her until their relationship grew. He was really looking forward to the hunt ball.

Although they had spoken on most days, Justin had not seen Hattie since the meeting as life as usual had been hectic. Her daughters had been to visit and he did understand that she didn't want to introduce him to them just yet.

It was the night of the ball and Justin had hired a black-tie outfit for the event. Hattie had told him she would be wearing a long dress. She also told him that her daughters had taken Fado on a holiday to Cornwall so she would not need a babysitter.

Justin had only one hope in his head as a result of this. Maybe he could stay the night with her.

A minibus was collecting them from the local pub and Hattie had insisted he meet her there as she could walk to it. The pub had agreed to people parking their cars overnight. Justin arrived early and ordered a pint. He recognised a couple of people from the stables and waved to them.

He was halfway through his pint when Hattie walked in. His heart missed a beat at her beauty. She was wearing a long red dress which highlighted her slim figure. Her wild auburn curls had been tamed into waves which curved around her beautiful rugged high cheek bones and down her elegant neckline. Her genuine open smile melted his resolve to keep his passion under his wrap until the end of the evening. He wrapped her in his arms and kissed her passionately on the lips telling her how beautiful she looked.

"Oh, Justin, control yourself in public! Although I must say, you scrub up well yourself."

Hattie pulled away from him breathlessly making light of his embrace as she observed the stable friends winking at her and muttering their surprise to each other.

She had not really spoken about the new man in her life with any of them.

After a quick glass of wine Hattie called to everyone that the minibus had arrived. There was much excited chatter on the journey to the venue of the ball. The hall was buzzing when they arrived and soon they were enjoying a delicious three course meal. Everyone was in high spirits as the promises auction got underway. Justin had his eye on a weekend for two at a bed and breakfast on Exmoor and without telling Hattie, he bid for it and won. He turned to Hattie who gave him a high five. He caught her hand and showered her arm with kisses.

When the live band began there was no hesitation and everyone leapt onto the dance floor. Hattie was the life and soul, head back in laughter as her feet moved with expertise to the beat. Justin was filled with admiration for this extraordinary and talented woman. She had a great sense of rhythm and seemed lost in the music.

His dancing skills left a lot to be desired but she took hold of him and made him lose all his inhibitions as they twirled around together.

When the band slowed the pace down by playing an old favourite, 'Lady in Red', Justin held Hattie in a tight embrace, kissing her neck as they swayed to the song.

All too soon the evening drew to a close and they were back in the minibus. Justin told Hattie he would take her back to the farm in his car as he had sobered up enough to drive up the lane. Hattie agreed with relief as her shoes were hurting her feet too much to walk. When they pulled up outside the farmhouse Justin leaned over and kissed Hattie not daring to hope that she would invite him in. They kissed lovingly until Hattie pulled away.

"It's a bit late for you to be driving home, you had better stay here."

"Well, I wouldn't turn an offer like that down."

Justin could hardly believe he was following Hattie up the double staircase of her beautiful house. She pulled him through the bedroom door and kissed him on the lips. He returned the kiss with vigour as he felt the stirring between his legs. He pushed her gently towards the bed as their lips remained locked. He lay her down on the bed and pulled her dress down finding to his surprise that she was not wearing a bra. He placed his tongue on her nipples twirling it around the perky little things whilst finding his way in between her legs with his hand.

To his pleasure, she had no pants on either and he felt her pleasure as he teased her precious parts with his fingers. She was moaning with pleasure. He was able to pull her dress down until her beautiful naked body lay underneath him and he managed to ease himself out of his suit with great speed. Soon they were entwined in the most exquisite ecstasy of love making.

Chapter 21

Hattie

The phone interrupted Hattie's lovely dream where she was galloping on a sandy beach with Justin at her side.

"Hello."

"Hi, it's Michelle; sorry to ring so early but John is at the stables. He was trying to get our pony and some of the others have pushed their way out of the field."

"OK, I am coming."

Hattie looked at the digital clock beside her bed. 5:30 a.m.

"Why on earth would anyone want to get their pony at this time?"

Hattie jumped out of bed forgetting for a moment the night before until she saw Justin lying on his back, one arm behind his head and one eye open. Her heart missed a beat.

"Oh, Justin, I am sorry. I have to deal with a crisis."

She leant over and kissed his forehead. He grabbed her face and kissed her on the lips. She didn't want to pull away but had no choice.

"Justin, the ponies are rampaging round the farm with an unknowledgeable pony owner. I really have to go."

"OK, I am coming with you. There must be something I can do to help."

Hattie was getting dressed as she looked out of the window. There was a full moon which lit up her large lawn revealing a group of ponies huddled under the willow tree. Willow was poisonous to horses and there were old grass cuttings under the tree which could cause colic if eaten by horses and this was a serious problem.

Hattie dashed outside and straight onto the lawn. She clapped her hands and shouted at the ponies to get off the lawn. They heard her and ran as she ran to open the gate, hoping they would go down the track towards their field. Hattie managed to grab hold of the livery pony's head collar. She talked to the little mare to calm her down and managed to get her in front of the other ponies and they dutifully followed them down to their field.

When she got to the gate she saw John the ponies' owner looking terrified at the gate. The big horses were there too snorting and stomping the ground. One of the bossy ponies put his ears back and launched himself at the horses as if to let them know that this was his field so keep out. The other ponies formed an orderly queue in their pecking order by the gate. Hattie opened the gate and they all followed it into the field.

Hattie shouted instructions to John and Justin to get some head collars for the horses from the stables. They ran off up the track, Hattie called to the horses and they turned their heads towards her. They had broken the fence down to escape.

She clapped her hands and shouted for them to go up the track. She hoped that they would either go back to their stables or the nearest field. She ran after them. They made their way to the stables and she shouted to John and Justin to open the stable doors. When she caught up with them they were all waiting to be let into their own stable and all three of them opened the doors for them to go in to safety.

"Wow, Hattie, that was pretty impressive, the horses and ponies just seem to know what you wanted them to do!"

Justin was amazed at Hattie's calm ability to deal with a whole herd of loose horses.

"Well, that's because I am their herd leader. So, John, what happened?"

"Err, Tatiana was too strong for me when I was leading her through the gate; she barged out opening the gate wide, then all the other ponies appeared and pushed past me."

"That doesn't explain how the horses got out or why they were all so fired up at this time in the morning."

"When I got to the yard there were two loose horses so I put them in the top field."

Hattie went to see which horses they were. To her surprise, they were the neighbours' horses, they must have got out of their field down the lane and fired all hers up. Hattie rang her neighbour who also found the fence broken at her horse field.

"Well, that's all sorted, time for breakfast I think."

Justin and Hattie said goodbye to John and went back to the farm.

"Hattie, you really are amazing with those horses."

"Yes, well, they don't call me the horse whisperer for nothing!" laughed Hattie.

Justin put his arm around her and kissed her. He didn't know what else to say to this extraordinary woman he was falling in love with. He felt exhausted but Hattie didn't seem affected by only having a few hours' sleep. He didn't know where she got her energy from.

Chapter 22

Fado

The day came when I was too big for my beloved Bubbles and I moved onto Sid, a Welsh section, A-show pony. Every weekend in the summer was spent on going to shows. I rode Sid in the showing classes and always got placed in the first three. Then I took Bubbles into the unridden showing class and we also did well. I loved to watch the older riders and learn from them.

Hattie spent the day running around after her pupils but she was always there to watch me in the show ring and I wanted to make her proud of me. At first, when Justin started to come along as well, I felt a little jealous and knew that I was being hostile towards him. I did not want to share Hattie's affections. After a while though, I couldn't help warming to him as he was good fun and always having a joke with me.

I found the transition to secondary school very hard. The bully boys at primary school had been caught out and stopped by the head teacher. The boys at secondary school were far more difficult to deal with. They made me realise how different I was. The other children had been born in Devon and were from totally different cultural backgrounds than me. It made me more aware of my origins and I really wanted to find out more about them. I dealt with the bullying by becoming a joker and won people's affections. However, my school work suffered whilst I was clowning around in class. The teachers were on at me to pay more attention. I got into trouble for not doing my homework all the time. I knew I wanted to work with horses and was only interested in the outdoor life. I loved art and all sport. Hattie made me have some private lessons in maths and English which I found very frustrating as it took me away from the stables. I became very interested in geography as I learnt about my birth country. I went to the computer club so that I could google all about Kenya. It was difficult for me to talk about this to Hattie. She was so kind and caring and I didn't want her to think I was ungrateful. But I knew that as soon as I could earn my own money I would go to Kenya and find my family.

There was a special hunt to be held at the kennels one Saturday. Hattie got Sheila to take over at the riding school and she said I could go with her on Sid. It would be our first hunt together and as Sid was a very fast pony, I couldn't wait. There was going to be a visiting hunt from up country. People had been asked to put up the visiting horses if they had spare stables but ours were full. It was a very big turnout. I counted forty horses and ponies at the meeting. I loved the sausages and homemade cake. I even tried a bit of mulled cider. I was chatting to my pony club friends when I spotted a horse from the visiting hunting party backing into my friend's dad on his horse. The rider cracked his whip and shouted abuse at them to get out of his way. It was at that moment when I recognised the loud abusive man. It was Tristan. I felt uncomfortable straight away and looked around for Hattie. She was off Crystal and helping to serve the port. Before I could say anything to her, the master was giving his speech and we were off.

We were in the woods where there were logs to jump over. Little Sid and I were having great fun going over the smaller logs when suddenly I heard a shout.

"Out of my way, boy."

It was Tristan thundering through the woods, his huge, grey horse dripping in sweat with its nostrils flared and ears back. I saw that he was heading for a fallen tree just beyond me. I made a quick decision to turn and go towards it cutting him off. I held onto the saddle as Sid leapt over a branch. Tristan's horse did an emergency stop rather than trying to jump me as well as the tree. He went flying over the horse's neck and landed on a spiked branch of the tree. He screamed in pain and swore in a very loud voice. I galloped off on Sid before anyone could blame me for the accident. Secretly I was really pleased with myself. Tristan deserved to fall off his poor horse. I remembered what a cruel and horrible man he was when he was our boss man in Kenya and clearly he still was. When I caught up with the master and the rest of the hunt who were on top of the hill watching the hounds at work, I told him that someone had fallen off in the woods. One of the riders offered to go back and see if he was OK. I found Hattie.

"Where have you been, young man?" she asked me.

"I was in the woods," I burst into tears, "Hattie, a man galloped towards me and then he fell off in the tree."

I didn't want to mention that it was Tristan and I knew I shouldn't have done that to him.

"Oh dear, well it's not your fault, so don't cry."

"Can we go home now, please?"

I wanted to leave before Tristan caught up with me.

"Of course, I was thinking it was about time we called it a day."

Thankfully, we got back to our horse box without bumping into Tristan.

I never told Hattie that I had caused the accident. I knew I shouldn't have got in his way but I just saw red and couldn't help myself.

A few weeks later it was the hunt ball. I hoped that Tristan wouldn't be there. I knew he wouldn't connect me to Hattie but he might have blamed me if he was relating the story and if he described me it would be obvious because of my colour.

Justin was taking Hattie. I loved to watch Hattie getting ready as she was transformed into a beautiful woman. People rarely saw Hattie dressed up.

The following day, Hattie was really tired. I made her a cup of tea and asked about the ball.

"Did you dance a lot?" I asked.

"Yes, the band was really good. Fado, I have to ask you about that accident on the visitors hunt."

"Oh, well I told you what happened on the day."

I was dreading what Hattie would say next.

"Tristan was relating the story to a group so loudly that everyone heard him."

Hattie looked stressed.

"He said that a coloured boy caused him to fall!"

"Did he? What else did he say?"

"He said that if he ever got hold of the little tyke, he'd horse whip him!"

Hattie looked at Fado and put a protective arm around Fado.

"Well, we'll just have to make sure he doesn't find the poor lad," I told Hattie with wink.

The day after the ball, Justin told me that he had won a day at a racing yard with a very well-known trainer and that I would be able to go. I was so excited. I had never been to a racing yard before but loved to watch the racing on TV. I had been to point to point as well and dreamt of riding one of those magnificent thoroughbreds one day.

The following Sunday Justin, Hattie and I set off for the day at the racing yard. The trainer was there to greet them and his wife invited them in for breakfast to meet their head jockey. The breakfast was just a boiled egg as jockeys couldn't eat much. I was still hungry after it. The trainer's wife offered to show Hattie around her house which was extremely old and haunted as it used to be a monastery. Rob the trainer and the jockey took Justin and I to the stables. The grooms were getting the horses ready for their morning exercise on the gallops. I was speechless at their beauty as I went up to a beautiful bright bay that put his head down and snorted at me.

"What is he called?" I asked.

"That one is Golden Boy, he has never been beaten," One of the jockeys told him.

"Wow, you are beautiful!" I told the horse.

They went along the row of stables meeting each of the horses and learning their racing story. I told Rob that I really wanted to be a jockey.

"Well, it's a hard life and sometimes dangerous, lad. I tell you what, why don't you come and spend a week here in your school holidays and see what you think after that?"

I could not believe my ears as I ran to find Hattie to tell her about this amazing offer.

Hattie was coming out of the house looking quite flushed, in a bit of a daze.

"Hattie, I have got some brilliant news!"

"Oh, just a minute, Fado, I have had quite an experience in the house. I need to come around from it."

"What do you mean?"

"Where is Justin. I need to tell him about the spirits I have been with in the house."

I was a bit shocked to hear this and worried that Hattie didn't seem herself. I decided that this was not the time to ask if he could accept Rob's offer of working at the yard. I took Hattie by the arm and led her to Justin who was watching the jockeys mount ready for the gallops.

"Hi, darling, how was your tour of the house?"

Justin put an affectionate arm round Hattie.

"I have had quite an experience encountering many spirits in the old house. It has an extremely sad story to tell about the days when the monks lived there."

Hattie leaned into Justin, glad to be back in her real life with the people she loved.

"I will look forward to hearing all about them, but for now, we must watch these magnificent horses at work."

I was in awe of the jockeys and really wished I was on one of the horses. I promised myself that as soon as I got back home I would practice riding my pony with very short stirrups.

The tour was over all too soon and I was shaking hands with Rob thanking him for the wonderful day.

"I expect I will see you again soon; just give us a ring when you can come for a week's work."

Hattie was surprised at this offer.

"Oh, that is very kind of you, Rob, Fado would love to spend a week with you in the summer holidays. He is not afraid of hard work either."

"Ha! Well, it will be hard work alright, but I like the kid's enthusiasm so just give me a ring."

They said their goodbyes and got into the car. I was beside myself with excitement.

"When can we fix a date?"

Hattie assured me we would look at the calendar as soon as we got home.

Chapter 23

Justin

Justin could not believe the whirlwind romance with Hattie. Things moved from nothing to full blown in no time. Hattie really knew her own mind. She didn't bother wasting time once it was made up. So, here they were two years into the relationship. He had just about finalised the legal guardian paperwork for Hattie regarding Fado which she and he were delighted about. He had managed to sever all contact with Tristan who did not want anything to do with Fado and was not interested in anyone connected to him.

The only thing preventing him from moving in with Hattie permanently was his past. Hattie had found out that he had been married and had children but not the truth about why they had split up. The discovery about the wife and children had nearly split them up.

It was a busy day at the riding school and Hattie had come in shattered. Justin and Fado had made spaghetti Bolognese. They all sat down for dinner and Hattie got up to get a drink. Justin's phone which was in the kitchen rang with a message.

Hattie picked it up and looked at it as she handed it to Justin. It was his youngest daughter Talia asking if he could do FaceTime.

"Who is Talia?" Hattie demanded.

"Hattie, I can explain."

"Fado, go and watch TV with your dinner please. Justin and I need to talk."

I did as I was told with a worried glance at Justin. He winked at me by way of saying don't worry.

"Well, what have you got to say for yourself? If you have been two timing me there will be no excuses accepted, we are finished."

"No, it's nothing like that. Talia is my daughter."

"Your daughter? How could we have been having a relationship all this time and I didn't know you had a daughter?"

"Oh, Hattie, please don't be upset with me. It's unforgiveable that I didn't tell you that I had been married with children. I just couldn't find the right time. I just didn't want to lose you. Please forgive me."

Hattie had not spoken to him for a week. Justin was heartbroken and didn't know what he could do to make it up to her. He had to contact her about the developments over Fado as she was applying to be his legal guardian. Justin requested a meeting as there were papers to sign. To his relief, as soon as they saw each other the chemistry between them overcame everything and they fell into each other's arms.

He had to gloss over the truth about why he split up with his wife. Hattie did question why he did not have much contact with his children. But for the time being things were fine again between them.

He felt Hattie would benefit from a holiday and came up with the idea of her and Fado doing some riding whilst he could go fishing. They were both very excited about this idea and chose a trip to Canada in August which was a very quiet month at the riding school.

******

After an exhausting week putting everything in order and preparing for the holiday it was a relief to be at the airport. There was no phone signal or Wi-Fi where we were heading in western Canada.

Hattie was a bit worried about that and hoped things would run smoothly without her. Millie and Ria were staying at the farm and Sheila assured her that everything would be fine at the stables.

Hattie slept for most of the twelve-hour flight to Vancouver. I watched films and played cards with Justin.

We had planned a whale watching trip when we arrived as we were not starting our adventure until the following morning.

We all put huge life-saving suits on and laughed at the sight of ourselves in them. We took photos of each other looking like Teletubbies. It was an open-air life boat type.

"Looks a bit flimsy to me," Hattie said accepting the driver's hand to help her get in.

"Ah, you'll be alright, ma'am, adds to the excitement being really close to the whales in my boat."

The man had a twinkle in his eye as he helped us all onto the boat. We bobbed up and down in the water as the boat went at great speed until we were far out at sea. At last, we slowed down and couldn't believe the sight before us. Nineteen killer whales surrounded us and some came really close to the boat flapping their huge tails. It was amazing to see them diving in and out of the water.

After the trip we enjoyed a lovely fish dinner on the waterfront and had an early night with the jet lag setting in. The next morning, we took a taxi to a small airport where the pilot was waiting to greet us. I was really excited to be getting on the small sixteen-seater plane and thrilled that the captain invited me to sit in the cockpit before take-off.

After an hour the plane landed on a grassy strip in the wilderness. Hattie, Justin and I were introduced to Jim the guide for the Goat Camp Pack trip which Hattie and I were going on. He was a softly spoken man of first nation origin. He wore a bandana around his long, dark and wavy hair. It took an hour to get to the lodge. Once we had been shown to the accommodation, I went off to explore. Hattie was happy to let me go as I was so excited and hyperactive. Justin got them both a drink of the port they had got at the airport and they collapsed on the sofa admiring the beautiful view of snow-capped mountains and lakes. Justin got his binoculars out.

"Oh my, what a beautiful place this is!" he exclaimed to Hattie.

"Can I have a look please?"

Justin handed the binoculars to Hattie.

"Wait a minute, is that a bear by the lake picking fruit off that bush?"

"What? Quick! Where is Fado?"

They both shot out of the lodge and ran in the direction of the lake. As they were approaching the horse coral, they spotted me. I was helping Dave the authentic cowboy who preferred to spend his time with the animals than with people. We were putting the hay out for the horses.

"We might have known that we would find you here," Justin called over to me.

"Hi, Fado, I see you have met the horses then. Which one have you chosen to ride?"

"Oh, Hattie, they are all so beautiful and there are some mares and foals in the coral over there."

I had the biggest smile on my face feeling so at home amongst all the horses.

"This is Dave. He is going to be our cook on the Goat Camp trip."

Dave gave Hattie and Justin a wave. His unshaven face looked weathered under his battered old cowboy hat.

"We came to find you because we saw a bear and we were worried for your safety," Justin told me.

Dave gave a chuckle and shook his head but carried on sharing the hay out.

"Wow! A bear let's go and find him!" I shouted as I ran out of the coral.

We all walked down to the main lodge by the lake. There was a group of people standing on the deck looking down at the long stretch of lawn towards the lake. A larger-than-life blonde American lady with a whisky in her hand beckoned us towards her and pointed down the garden.

Hattie, Justin and I all gasped as we saw a huge grizzly standing at full height by the trees. He was picking blueberries from the surrounding bushes. Kim, the owner of the resort came out and told us that it was the best time of year for the blueberries.

"Follow me out the back if you want to see our black bears."

The guests all followed her through the lodge to the other side. Just as they got to the door, one of the dogs was barking. They couldn't believe their eyes as a black bear, being chased by the dog, nearly knocked me flying as I stepped out of the doorway. Everyone ran out to see the dog chase the bear down the drive and over the fields.

"The beggars steal food from our bins," Kim told us. "The dogs chase them off."

The blonde American put her arm round me.

"Gee, that was a close call, honey! Are you OK?"

I went red in the face embarrassed by the lady who introduced herself as Suzy and had a very loud voice with a North Carolina accent.

With all the excitement everyone was ready for a drink before settling down to a delicious lunch of salad and homemade cheese pie. After lunch we met with the stable girls and were allocated horses for the afternoon ride. Justin went down to the lake to meet with the other fishermen and the riders were taught how to tack up the western style; then we enjoyed a lovely ride.

We had been back an hour and were all having a pre-dinner drink with lots of exciting chatter about the horses and fishing, when the heavens opened and there was a terrible storm which lasted several hours. Jim gave the riders the bad news that they would not be able to set off on the Goat Camp trail the next day.

I was very disappointed at this news.

"Not to worry, darling. We can ride out from here and then go for a swim, go canoeing and go in the hot tub," Hattie reassured us.

"Yes, I will join you for the activities on the lake in the afternoon."

Justin joined in enthusiastically.

I felt a bit happier after hearing about the day's activities at the lodge. One of the stable girls came up to me whilst the others were finishing their coffee.

"Hey, would you like to come and help bring the horses down?"

The girl put her arm on my shoulder. I jumped up without hesitation and followed her out.

The next day was hot and sunny with no more storms. Jim told them that they would be setting off tomorrow.

The group were given rucksacks to pack which the pack horses would carry. The riders were given an early breakfast. We got our own horses ready and then watched Jim and Dave load the pack horses. It was a very skilful job to make sure that the horses' load was evenly packed to make them as comfortable as possible. At last, everyone was ready to leave. All the staff and other lodge guests came to wave us off on our adventure.

The trail on the first day was a very difficult one. We rode through dense mountain forests. At some points, the trail had been blocked by fallen trees after the storms. Jim had to ride along with a chain saw across his saddle to clear the way. Hattie and I were riding near the back as they were not leading pack horses. I had a little Paint horse called Chico who liked to jog along. Hattie had an Arab cross who was very forward going and didn't really like being at the back. We both had trouble keeping their horses still whilst waiting for the trail to be cleared. Sometimes we would be standing on a very steep track. Hattie had to use her soothing voice to calm herself and the horse. There were fast flowing streams to cross. The more sensible horses walked through them carefully. Mine and Hattie's horses preferred to jump them.

The worst part of the trail was getting through the bogs. They hadn't gone far when they came across one. The lead riders with their pack horses seemed to get through OK. Abby's horse was in front of Hattie's when he started sinking.

"Abby, your horse is sinking! Quick, grab that tree to get yourself off!"

Abby was screaming as she felt her horse going down into the bog right up to the top of his tail. Somehow, she managed to do as Hattie said and pull herself off. The horse, free of his burden was able to get through the bog.

"Loose horse," I shouted, used to the warning from hunting.

"Can somebody help us, please?" shouted Abby, still clinging to the tree.

Hattie and I had a job to keep our horses back as they were now left behind with the rest of the herd gone. To our relief, Jim and Dave appeared with Abby's horse and the chain saw. After helping her back on, they cleared another trail for Hattie and I and everyone was soon reunited.

After a ten-hour ride the group finally arrived at the campsite. Everyone helped to get the load off the pack horses. Next, we untacked and fed our own horse. Finally, we could pitch our tents and enjoy the Mexican wraps and toasted marshmallows around the campfire cooked by Dave. We all slept until dawn, exhausted by our adventurous day. The next few days were spent leisurely riding up and down the surrounding mountains. We picnicked on the top viewing eagles, mountain goats and bears through our binoculars.

All too soon, it was time to take the trail back again. Thankfully, we only had to ride five hours to the lagoon where Bud, the lodge owner, collected us by boat. To our surprise, the horses were sent home from there on their own. I worried that my lovely little horse, Chico, would be attacked by a bear. We all watched out for our horses to return when we were back at the lodge. We feared for our horses' safety. Six hours after we had let them go, the horses, led by my little paint, came trotting into the lodge yard. We all cheered and ran to pat our horses. Dave led them into the coral where their hay was waiting for them.

Hattie turned to give Justin a hug with tears in her eyes.

"This was a truly amazing experience. Out there in the wilderness, at one with nature, is where I feel at peace with myself."

"Yes I know, darling, and that is why I love you so much."

I helped Dave to settle the horses before we all enjoyed our last supper.

It took a few weeks before Hattie could settle back down to the reality of life at the stables. The experience of the holiday had done her the world of good. For me, it was a life-changing experience. Like Hattie, I knew where I felt most at home. Out in the wilderness, at one with nature.

Justin was so pleased that the holiday had been such a success. He began staying with Hattie more often and their relationship grew stronger.

Chapter 24

Fado

"Wow, are we really going to Canada?"

I was jumping up and down with the brochure in my hand.

"These photos look amazing. We might even see bears!"

The photos of the place they were going to looked just like the country where the western movies were filmed. I watched the old movies over and over. I liked to study the way the Indians behaved with their horses. When the film had finished, I would go out and try some new training techniques on my ponies. So, to actually go on a holiday where these places were filmed was a dream come true.

"Will we see any Indians, Hattie? I love the way they have a special relationship with their horses."

"The lodges we will be staying in are on an Indian reservation. I think the owner is of Native American Indian origin," Justin told me.

"That is just amazing. I'm going to love being with these people and their horses."

I ran off to tell the girls at the stables.

It was a truly magical experience. I had a beautiful quarter horse. I felt I had a strong sense of telepathy with my horse; I was at one with nature itself. I was very sad when the trail ride was over and we had to leave the wilderness camp. We actually came very close to the bears. One morning, I was desperate for the toilet and had to climb out of the tent at dawn. I was making my way down to a bush when I heard a bell. The horses had bells on them at night to warn the bears off. I froze fearing there might be one close by. I wrapped myself around a tree trunk hoping to hide. Suddenly, I felt something sticky on my hands. It was the tree sap which was oozing out of the trunk after the bear had scratched it. I peered from behind the tree to see if the coast was clear. I held my breath as there was a black bear over by the table. He was rummaging in the black sack for food. I was so scared but knew I just couldn't move for fear of him seeing me. Suddenly, the bell was ringing again and the bear fled as the horses returned to camp for their breakfast. Our guide Josh was getting out of his tent.

"What are you doing clung to that tree, lad?" he asked as he spotted me.

"I, err, saw the bear over there, I wanted the toilet."

"Oh, you mean the cheeky rubbish raider, well, you've frightened him off now, so off you go."

After that I never got out of the tent on my own again.

When we got back from Canada there was an answerphone message from Rob, the racehorse trainer. I had to play the message over a few times before I could believe what it said.

"Hi, Mrs Gee, it's Rob here. I was just wondering if that lad of yours is free to spend next week with us?"

"Oh, please can I go Hattie?" I pleaded.

I had been nagging her to go all summer. Hattie had said she didn't like to bother the busy trainer.

"Well, I suppose as he has actually rung up and asked for you to go, he must really mean it. Although, I do worry, it's a very dangerous sport, you know. I don't want you having any accidents."

"I promise I'll keep out of trouble," I pleaded.

"OK, but you need to be very careful."

Hattie gave in.

"Yes!"

I waved my fist in the air and ran upstairs to start packing.

"Just a minute, I have hardly finished doing the washing from Canada. Let's look at the calendar and see which would be the best day for you to go, before I ring Rob back."

We decided on the Monday which was a quiet day at the stables with no extra riders. Hattie rang Rob.

"Hi, Rob, it's Hattie here."

"Hello. You got my message then?"

"Yes and Fado is very keen. Would Monday be OK for him to come to you?"

"Yes, Monday will be fine. Will it be OK if he sleeps above the stables with the other jockeys?"

Hattie laughed as she assured him I would love to sleep with the horses.

On Monday morning I was up at the crack of dawn, bags packed and waiting by the front door. I dashed out to the stables to say goodbye to my favourite ponies.

When I got back to the house, Hattie had a huge farmhouse breakfast waiting for me.

"Remember how hungry we were after the light breakfast at the racing yard?" Hattie reminded me.

"Oh yes, I forgot they are all on diets so that they do not carry too much weight in their races. I will make the most of it, thanks."

I began shovelling the ham, eggs and beans into my mouth at speed.

"Steady on there, lad, you'll have indigestion for the journey."

Justin patted me on the shoulder as he walked over to the sink to fill the kettle.

"I'll go out and see if Sheila needs anything before we go. Justin, can you tidy up and then we'll be ready to take off when I get back."

"Will do, my love, Fado can help. We are going to miss him this week."

With all the bags in the car, they were on the road by nine o'clock. It took a couple of hours to get there which went very quickly as I couldn't stop chatting with excitement all the way. Rob was there to greet them with one of the stable hands who showed me where to put my bags. Hattie and Justin were invited into the house for a coffee whilst I went straight to the yard duties.

Hattie and Justin had no worries about leaving me an hour later. When they came to say their goodbyes, they found me flattening the muckheap with a huge grin on my face.

I loved every part of the work I was given to do.

My favourite task was grooming the racehorses. Their coats shone when I had finished. Not all the horses enjoyed being handled and groomed. Some would snort and flatten their ears at me. Some would stamp their front feet when I opened the stable door.

"Watch out for grumpy chops over there!" shouted Johnny as I opened Silver Starr's stable door.

"She is one moody mare, that one," Johnny warned.

"Hey, it's OK there, my beauty." I spoke to her in a soft quiet voice whilst lowering my head so as not to appear threatening.

The mare raised her head and snorted.

"It's OK now." I whispered turning my back on her and standing very still.

The mare stamped her foot and flattened her ears. Most of the other stable hands would be making their escape by this time and I stood motionless. After a few moments, I could hear the mare licking and chewing. I turned my head slightly and could see that she was lowering hers. As I turned towards her, she decided to munch her hay.

"Good girl, no need to worry now."

I reached up to rub Starr's neck. She carried on eating her hay. I was able to give the mare a good grooming without any further trouble.

"Wow! I have never seen her behave like that before. What did you do, drug her?"

Johnny was genuinely impressed.

"Oh, it was nothing, she just got bored of being bad," I told Johnny.

Soon it was all around the yard that Fado had done what even Rob couldn't do with the mare.

"Hey, lad, perhaps you'd like to take her on the gallops tomorrow morning?" Rob suggested.

"What? You really think I could?"

"Yes please."

I couldn't wait for the morning. I got up really early to spend extra time with Silver Starr before tacking her up. She went through the snorting, stamping and ears back motions. However, she soon dropped her head when I managed to breathe up her muzzle. I spent a long time grooming her and then tacked her up. By the time I got her out of the stable, the sun was up and they joined the others at the mounting block. Rob strode purposefully towards them.

"This is a very valuable horse, lad. Not many people can get on with her so she doesn't get to go out much. You ride her well and who knows, maybe you'll be her next jockey."

He gave Fado a leg up. I felt my legs shaking as I so hoped that I could ride Silver well enough.

"Stick with me, lad. I'll set the pace and you won't have to worry."

I was relieved to hear Johnny's friendly voice and I stopped shaking.

"We can do this, my little Starr," I spoke softly to her whilst gently rubbing her neck.

We all rode out to the gallops and Rob sent them off two by two. I felt the wind rushing through my ears as Starr glided through the air.

They galloped round the track three times when Johnny shouted, "Sit back, we need to slow down."

"OK, I'll try, but we are going so fast. I'm not sure I can stop."

I had no idea how I was going to get Starr to slow down. When I sat back I nearly lost my balance as the stirrups were so short. I panicked as my feet came out of them. I wrapped my legs around Starr clinging on with all my weight on her as

I sat deep in the saddle. She didn't stop with the others and carried on when everyone else stopped.

I was contemplating bailing out as I didn't know how much longer I could hang on.

"Try and sit up, lad."

Johnny had caught up with me again.

"I'm trying!" I shouted.

I grabbed my right rein as I suddenly remembered Hattie once telling me that this was a good way of slowing down a bolting horse. I put my other hand on the horse's neck and pushed myself upright. With my legs tightly wrapped around Star's belly I felt her begin to slow down. Unfortunately, we were heading for a tree as we were going off the gallops. Starr swerved the tree preventing an injury however she left me behind as I landed with a thud on the tree roots.

"Are you OK, lad?"

Johnny was off his horse and helping me up.

"I think so." I said seeing stars as I had banged my head on the tree.

Rob came up to us holding a very sweaty and snorting Star.

"What happened? Did you lose control?"

"He just got faster and faster," I told Rob near to tears, "I'm really sorry."

"Well, maybe we were a bit premature letting you loose on the gallops; you've a bit more work to do with this horse yet."

I felt better hearing that I was going to have another chance with Starr. My pride was hurt as well as my head, but I certainly wasn't ready to give up yet.

I gave Starr a rub telling her I knew it wasn't her fault. I took Starr back and washed her down before tucking her up into her stable.

I rang Hattie to tell her about the exciting day that I had. I made light of the fall.

"What do you mean you bumped into a tree?"

"Well, Starr managed to swerve it but I didn't," I tried to explain.

"Are you sure, you're OK?"

Hattie was worried.

"You may have concussion."

"I'm sure, I'm fine, I'll be more careful next time," I reassured her.

"Oh, please be careful, Fado, we don't want you in hospital and the social workers onto us again."

"Oh, Hattie, please try not to worry, I really love it here."

I knew Hattie did worry about me but she also understood that I had a passion which I share with her; she would support me.

I had a restless night of dreams as I was galloping the hills and on the beach on Silver Starr. The next day was my last and I really wanted to try the gallops again on Starr. Rob wasn't keen to allow me to but I pleaded with him.

"OK, but go on the short circuit first with Johnny."

"Thank you so much, I'll be really careful."

I was so pleased that Rob had given me another chance.

Johnny and I set off at a steady pace side by side and completed the circuit.

"Can we have a go on the long one now?" I asked Johnny.

"Well, the calm manner in which I put her food in seems to have worked."

Johnny nodded as we headed for the long track.

I was careful to stay light in the saddle and keep Starr at a steady pace behind Johnny and his horse. This time we arrived back safely.

"Oh, thank you so much, Johnny, I'm so happy to have done the gallops on Starr before I leave tomorrow."

I realised that it was a dangerous sport training race horses and I would have to always be ready for the unpredictable.

I was determined to come back for the next holidays. I knew that I definitely wanted to be a jockey and wished I was sixteen so that he could start training for my license.

Chapter 25

Hattie

Hattie had enjoyed the holiday immensely. She had not had a holiday since the horseback safari six years ago. This was also a life-changing holiday in that she had some breath-taking experiences. The time in the bush had been where Hattie felt she belonged to and likewise the time camping in the wilderness at one with nature felt like home to her. It took a while to bring her back down to earth. The hustle and bustle of life when she got back was difficult to get involved in.

Fado was very excited about the work experience at the racing yard. Hattie smiled to herself at how fickle teenagers were. She remembered how her three at that age had the ability to move from one thing to the next with surprising ease, living for the moment, never mind the consequences.

With Fado away for the week, she had time to organise things for the start of the new term at the riding school. She told Justin that she needed a little space after the holiday. She felt dreadful about this given the fact that he had booked and paid for it. However, she had not had time to process the fact that he had not been entirely truthful to her throughout their relationship. The fact that she had found out by chance was that he was married and had children. What else was he hiding from her? She decided to ring and invite her daughters down for a few days.

"Hi, Mum, we're here."

Ria and Millie both arrived together and ran to hug their mother.

"Oh, Mum, I can't believe we've got a few days alone together with no other distractions."

Ria looked beautiful in her long boots and leggings.

"Can we go to the spa and have afternoon tea as a rare treat?"

Millie as ever wanted to organise the activities.

"Okay, we can do that tomorrow. Tonight, I have made us a pasta bake and we can have a good catch up with a couple of glasses of wine."

Hattie was so pleased to have her girls to herself. She had not been separated from Fado since the day she had found him. She worried that he would be taken care of at the racing yard but it was lovely not to have the responsibility. As the evening wore on, Hattie became relaxed with her daughters and with perhaps a little too much wine she found herself revealing all her concerns about Justin.

"Mum, all we have to do is Google him. We can find out everything about him."

Ria had the iPad at the ready.

"Tell me about your relationship, Mum. Are you very fond of him?" Millie, the more analytical, stressed the importance of this and whether she really wanted to know more about him.

Hattie told the girls all the positive things about Justin. The more she revealed the more she realised how very fond of him she was.

"The trouble is, how can the relationship progress if I am not sure about his past?"

"Well, you have been seeing him for a while without his past affecting you," Ria pointed out.

They ended up putting his name into Google. They didn't find out much more than they already knew. It did not explain why he left Africa on his own separated from his wife and family.

"Okay. You just need to talk to him about your concerns," Ria as ever the practical one told her.

"I will girls, don't worry about it. What will be will be," Hattie reassured her girls.

"Mum, you do seem very relaxed after your holiday. Tell us all about it. Have you got the photos?"

Millie was always observant of any changes in her mother.

The rest of the evening was spent showing photos and Hattie telling the girls about the wonderful holiday Justin had taken her on.

The next day after checking in at the stables and having a ride out with Ria, the three of them spent the afternoon at the spa. The days with her daughters went all too quickly for Hattie and it was time for them to return to their city lives.

After receiving the excited phone call from Fado just after the girls left, Hattie had an overwhelming need to contact Justin and tell him all the news. They met for dinner at the local pub.

"Oh, Hattie, I have missed you so much these last few days. Please tell me if I have done anything wrong?"

Justin looked drawn and anxious.

"I just wanted to spend some time alone with my daughters," Hattie told him by way of an excuse as she felt sorry for his anxiety over her.

He was clearly very fond of her.

"Of course, I can understand that."

He gave a sigh of relief.

Hattie plucked up courage to tell him how she felt.

"It's just that, sometimes I get worried that I don't really know you. I mean I know and love you as you are, but I don't know or understand your past."

"Oh, Hattie," Justin said taking hold of her hands. "I have adored you from the day I met you. I know I have been reluctant to tell you about my past for fear of losing you. That was so wrong of me and I know that now. I was married and do have two children."

"Life was difficult for us in Africa during the last few years and we argued a lot. Things got really bad between us and my wife walked out one day whilst I was at work. She took our two children and returned to her family in Austria. When I returned from work, she had gone without even leaving a note. I was frantic. I didn't know if they were safe or if they had been abducted. Finally, after weeks of research I found out where they were. My wife told me never to contact her or my children again. It's only now, years later that my daughter has found me on Facebook and wants to get back in touch with me. There has been no contact with my son."

Tears were rolling down Hattie's face as Justin told his story.

"Well of course you must get back in touch with your daughter."

"Yes I really want to."

"I will support you. I don't know what I would do if any of my children lost touch with me. But this still doesn't explain why she left you."

"I have trouble understanding that myself. She just didn't like life in Kenya. It was so culturally different from her upbringing in Switzerland."

Justin was relieved that Hattie seemed to accept this explanation without further questions. He wanted to meet up with his daughter and did not want it to be a secret.

"I am going to try and arrange to meet her in the next school holidays. She is fifteen now and can travel on her own. Would you be happy to meet her?"

Justin was hoping they could make the reunion together as Hattie could change any awkward situation into a relaxing one.

"Well, no, Justin. You must meet her on your own for the first time. Then perhaps we can all get together once you have broken the ice. Fifteen-year-olds can be very sensitive. You can say or do the wrong thing and that would be the end of that. Just meet on a neutral ground together and take it from there. How about taking her Christmas shopping in London?"

Justin knew Hattie was right. Judging by her Facebook page his daughter loved to keep up with the latest fashions.

"Thanks, Hattie, you always know the right thing to do."

Hattie had her own problems to deal with. She loved Christmas and wanted to be surrounded by all her family. She had the ideal place to host everyone; a huge tree in the hall, fresh evergreen and ivy draped around the farmhouse. Cakes and puddings had to be made six weeks before. It was a time for all the traditions to be carried on as her family had done.

However, this year, Millie was saying that she would have to go to her fiancé's family. Ria was saying that she and her boyfriend were undecided what to do as he was an only child and his parents had no one else. Her son had said that he was happy to have her up to stay with him in London. His wife did not want to leave her family. This made Hattie very sad. She could not go away as there was no one to look after the farm. She made that quite clear to everyone and really hoped that they would all decide to come to the farm.

Hattie also worried about Fado. He had clearly been very successful at the racing yard and couldn't wait to get back there. This was all very well but she really wanted him to try and get some qualifications before leaving school.

"But, Hattie, all the other jockeys left school at sixteen. They haven't even got any GCSE's!"

"That may be, but you can't be a jockey for the rest of your life. You may want to be an accountant when you're forty."

"I will never want to do anything but work with horses. The other jockeys earn good money."

The only thing he read was The Racing Post. He hated school and was not doing very well at all in any academic subject. It upset Hattie to see him so unhappy. She felt she was being hard on him. Lots of boys of his age were not motivated to do anything. Fado was very motivated when it came to his chosen career. Part of her wanted to push him academically so that he would have something to fall back on if he failed as a jockey. Some days, she felt as if she should just let him go for it whilst he was young and able. Hattie promised Fado that they would make a decision after Christmas.

By the end of November, Hattie's wishes had come true. All the children would be with her for some of the Christmas

168

period. Ria and Millie on Christmas day and her son on Boxing Day. They also made a plan to celebrate her birthday with her on New Year's Eve. Hattie was so happy and really looking forward to the festive season. The stables had to be organised as the horses did not know it was Christmas. She was determined that Sheila should take the time off with her family. With Ria now having other commitments, she feared that all the work would be left to her and Fado.

How wrong she was!

"Hattie, would you like the girls and I to come up early on Christmas morning and help you?" June asked her.

"Oh, that is so kind of you. I want to give Sheila the day off and was so worried what I was going to do."

Hattie loved the Willow family. They had done so well with their young horse and were always willing to help out around the yard.

"Millie and Ellie have said they'll be up early as well."

June didn't mind an early start at the stables with her girls as her boys wouldn't get up till late.

"Brilliant. We'll have everything done in no time with all hands-on deck."

Hattie was delighted at the offers of help. It was a real weight off her shoulders.

Hattie was going to surprise Fado with a membership for the Jockey Club for Christmas. This would enable him to apply to go to the jockey school where he could go on a course during the school holidays and get his license. This way, she could keep him at school for another year at least. He could take his GCSE's and be qualified as a jockey for the following season. She had given Rob a ring and followed his advice on this. He had told her that Fado could begin his job at the racing

169

yard as soon as his exams were over. She decided not to have any more arguments with Fado about his education. When he nagged her about it, she would just tell him to, 'Wait and see.'

There was another surprise for everyone this Christmas. Hattie had a phone call from her son Simon. He wanted to come to the farm for a few days including Christmas Day. Hattie was so excited as he rarely came to the farm. It was her dream to have all three of her children together. This had rarely happened since they had become adults with their own busy lives to deal with. It had worked out well that Justin was not going to be with them as Simon could get a bit jealous if she showed affection towards any other man whilst he was with her. It would be difficult enough with Fado there.

On Christmas Eve, Hattie got up at six to make sure everything was done at the stables. There were lots of jobs to do in the house preparing for her three children arriving. Hattie was really looking forward to a happy family Christmas with them all.

With all the food prep done, presents wrapped and wood burner lit, Hattie was having a glass of port by the fire when her son arrived.

"Hi, Mum, I'm so excited to be at the farm for Christmas."

"Lovely to have you here as well."

Hattie gave Simon a hug.

"Oh good, I'm first here, I've got you all to myself for a change."

"Shall I get you a beer?"

Hattie hoped that Fado wouldn't get in from the stables just yet so that she could spend a little time alone with her son. She knew he wanted her individual attention and would get

170

upset if anyone interrupted the precious time. They were chatting by the fire with their drinks when Fado burst in.

"I'm freezing, lovely to see the fire."

Fado went to sit on the hearth, warming his hands. Hattie felt her son's tension.

"You've been out all day in the cold, why don't you go and get in the bath to warm up, after saying hi to Simon?"

"Oh, hi, Simon, when did you arrive?"

"Only about half an hour ago, I was just having a nice chat to mum."

If Fado felt the cold reception from Simon he didn't show it and was his usual bright and positive self.

"Great to see you, I'll go and change out of my horsey clothes; sorry if I'm a bit smelly."

"That would be a good idea as I'm allergic to horses, you know."

Fado gave Hattie a puzzled look. She'd never mentioned that Simon was allergic to horses.

"Oh dear, I'll go and scrub myself in the bath then."

Fado ran out of the room taking the stairs two at a time.

"He's still a live wire then. How are you getting on with finding his family?" Simon asked Hattie with some hostility.

"Well, you had lots of energy at his age. I'm afraid, we haven't been able to find his family yet."

"So, what is your plan for his future?"

Simon wanted to know.

"He wants to be a jockey; he's already spent some time with a trainer."

"Oh good, at least he'll be off your hands soon then."

Hattie wanted to change the subject and really hoped that her son's hostility towards Fado wasn't going to spoil Christmas.

"How are you getting on at work? Congratulations on your promotion."

Simon happily told Hattie all about work. The girls arrived together an hour later bringing life and laughter to the house with their funny stories about their lives. Christmas was a very happy time with all the family together. Simon seemed to relax and enjoy being with his sisters.

Fado made everyone laugh with his magic shows and gymnastic displays. The festive period was over all too soon.

Chapter 26

Justin

Justin was sad and disappointed that he could not spend Christmas with Hattie. However, he was so looking forward to seeing his daughter. They had met in London during her school holidays for the past year. Justin loved her very much. She was vivacious, kind and intelligent. He was very sad that his son did not choose to see him. He could understand that his wife would not communicate with him. It was unforgivable the way he sent those poor prisoners to work on the drug farms. They had to work so hard out in the heat with little food or water. Understandably, when his wife had found out what he was doing she took the children and left.

He just wished that he could see his son and try and make amends for all the years they had been apart.

On the drive to London, he was deep in thought; his past haunting him as always when he was alone. He felt really lucky to have met Hattie who loved him for the person he was without a sordid past. He prayed that she never found out.

Luckily, there were no hold ups and he was early for Talia. He got himself a coffee and waited on the platform for her train to come in. As soon as he saw his beautiful daughter running towards him all his troubles disappeared.

Justin and Talia had great fun in London for Christmas; their three days together flew past and he was putting her back on the train for Heathrow.

He phoned Hattie as soon as he hit the road and they had a long chat catching up about their Christmas breaks without each other. By the time he reached Devon, they had spoken on the hands free most of the way and he couldn't wait to see her. They arranged to have dinner together that evening. Hattie had had a fun-filled hectic Christmas with all her family to cater for and looking after all the horses in between. Justin was determined to care for her over the next few days. He wasn't much good with the horses although he did try to help with the heavy duties at the yard.

He had plans for New Year's Eve that he really hoped Hattie would agree to. He had booked for the two of them to spend the evening at a country house hotel and stay the night. It was only twenty minutes from where they lived but he felt it was important to have the quality time together. Having checked with Fado who had told him he was staying with one of his jockey friends, Sheila was able to cover the yard duties on New Year's Day.

He would tell Hattie about the plans this evening.

Justin arrived at the farm in time to help settle the horses for the night. He left Hattie finishing off and went with Fado to start the dinner. Hattie had prepared a cottage pie earlier that morning so it was just the vegetables to prepare and turning the oven on. Justin loved to light the wood burner and enjoy a cosy evening at the farm with Hattie. They were like an old married couple. If only Hattie would accept the ring. He decided not to ask her again on New Year's Eve. If she declined again it would ruin the evening and the next day. He realised he would just have to be happy with their relationship and not want more.

When they were sat around the table with the delicious warming cottage pie, Justin took the opportunity to tell of his plans for New Year's Eve.

"Got any ideas about New Year's Eve?"

Justin winked at Fado as he asked Hattie.

"Sleeping," sighed Hattie.

"Ah well, how would you like to go to The Stag for dinner and stay the night? It's peaceful enough there for a good night's sleep."

Justin hoped she would agree.

"No, I couldn't leave the stables. No one gets up on New Year's Day. I have to feed and turn up." Hattie sounded disappointed.

"It's OK, Sheila has agreed to cover you. Go on, Hattie, it will be great for you to have a little break."

Justin was grateful for Fado's input.

"OK, that sounds like the best idea yet. I'll check with Sheila tomorrow."

Hattie kissed Justin as she got up to clear the plates.

"Thanks, love, that's a lovely idea."

They really enjoyed the New Year celebrations at the Stag dancing the night away. The dinner was very special. Justin was so happy when Hattie told him how much she loved him. That night in the vast four-poster bed, they made passionate love before falling asleep wrapped in each other's arms. Justin hoped they would be together forever. Hattie told Justin that she loved having him in her life and couldn't imagine being without him.

They discussed Fado and how they would support him in his fast-moving career as a jockey. He was doing very well and both Justin and Hattie helped Fado financially.

Chapter 27

Fado

It seemed a long time ago that I was hanging around Starr's neck on that first race up the gallops. It was only a couple of years but a lot had happened.

Thinking back to the time when Hattie found me down the badger set on her farm, the years have flown by. I am very lucky to be where I am today. No one expected me to get this far considering how frightened of horses I was when Hattie first took me to her stables. Now, I was working my way up to being a successful jockey.

I didn't share my past with many people. Not even Hattie knew that my driving ambition was to earn enough money to find my family in Kenya and help them. I often felt guilty about the rich lifestyle I was leading compared to my family. We had no running water or food from supermarkets full of food where I came from. What little money I was earning went into my savings account for them. If I could win a big race like the Gold Cup then I would have enough to go. Now that I was eighteen I could arrange the trip myself.

When I first saw Raven's beauty snorting and kicking his way down the ramp, I never imagined what lay ahead. The horse was given to me to care for as he was notoriously tricky. He didn't trust anyone, particularly men.

I used all the natural horsemanship skills to get close to the beautiful dark bay with his gleaming coat. I rang Hattie for advice.

"Hi, Hattie. I have been given a real beauty to work on. Trouble is, I can't get near him."

"Lovely to hear from you. I wish you would ring more often! Anyways not to worry, I know you're very busy with the training."

"Sorry, Hattie, by the time I finish in the evening, I'm shattered and I'm on the gallops at six in the morning."

"I know, love, I'm really proud of you."

"Thanks. What shall I do about Raven? I can't start working with him because he just puts his ears back and lurches at me teeth bared."

"Oh dear, he sounds very frightened!"

"Yes, he's obviously had a bad experience with people."

"Well, to start with, do not face him. Approach with your eyes down and hands behind your back. Talk in a low soothing voice. Standing to the side of the stable door at first, open it and do the same just inside the stable."

"Thanks, Hattie. I promise I'll keep in touch and let you know how I get on."

"Please do and I hope to be at your first race with him."

After a few months, Raven had finally stopped putting his ears back whenever I approached the stable. He obediently backed up when I put my hand up before opening the door. Alongside the improving groundwork, I was able to mount him without so much fuss. At first, I had landed on the floor numerous times as Raven had spun around and shot off before

I could get into the saddle. With a lot of careful and patient training at the mounting block, I could now get on. However, he would only accept me being given a leg up if it was by a girl.

I had been racing on Starr, getting placed several times. Rob knew I was a good jockey and was prepared to be patient where Raven was concerned. He had accepted the horse on the condition the owner did not push to have him raced before his training program had been completed. The horse had gone for a reasonable price at the sale despite being highly bred. The owner didn't realise that because he was virtually impossible to handle.

Rob was very fond of me and thought I had a special talent with his horses, both on and off them. He had given me the unusual role of handling, training and racing certain horses.

I loved my work in spite of having plenty of knocks and bruises. The horses I was given to work with were not easy but I knew their behaviour was only this way because of fear. Training racehorses was still mostly old-fashioned in its methods. Most people's aim was to get the horse racing as young as possible. A horse bolts out of fear and some young horses do just that on the racecourse. However, this is at a price. The poor animals are so frightened that they fight all efforts to handle them.

Rob built me a round pen to work the horses in. He was very impressed at how many hours I spent with them. He sometimes watched me working on the horses.

"That's just amazing, lad. I've never seen anything like it!" Rob shouted as he watched me.

I would stand in the middle of the pen with the horse racing around the outside. Bucking, kicking, snorting and working up a sweat. Eventually, he would stop, head in the air and his nostrils flared. At this signal I would turn my back.

"Very impressive!" Rob would call out as he watched the horse lower his head.

Sometimes he sniffed and pawed the ground before slowly making his way towards me. I kept very still, head down and back turned until I felt a nuzzle on my shoulder. That was my signal to turn and rub his neck before putting the head collar on him.

"There's a good lad, nothing to worry about now." I would whisper.

From this point on, the horse would follow me around at the end of the rope without resistance, stop when I stopped, and trotted when I ran.

"Brilliant, Fado," my other jockey and trainer mates would shout as they gathered around the edge of the round pen amazed at what they saw.

After this training in the round pen, which took several sessions to get to the point where the horse trusted me, I could do most things without a battle.

"Trouble is, it's only you he'll trust," Johnny pointed out.

"Well, why don't you come in and give it a go?" I encouraged my friend.

He gave it a go and sometimes the horse would submit but other times he wouldn't leave my side.

I didn't mind this because it meant that they were mine to handle.

At last, the day arrived when I was taking Raven to his first race. I spent time massaging and grooming him to relax him before going in for breakfast.

"Rob, who is going to walk Raven around?"

"Jenny will be the best for the job."

"Will she be able to give me a leg up?"

"Of course, she will. Now, what are you going to take to settle your nerves?"

"OK, OK, I'm just checking everything is   sorted."

"I know, lad, it's a very important day for you."

We all liked Jenny as she had a good and calm influence over the horses.

"Thanks, Jenny will help me to calm my nerves."

I was nervous but knew I could not show the horse. I took deep breaths on the way to the stable. Raven backed up when he saw his master and his ears were pricked forward. I wondered if he had any idea about the big event he was about to go to. I breathed a sigh of relief as they lifted the ramp on the lorry. I was surprised that he had walked straight in with me.

When we arrived at the races it was still fairly quiet. I had deliberately got there early to keep Raven calm before his race which was the third one of the days.   He settled down with some hay in the makeshift stable. I asked Jenny to keep an eye on him whilst I went to find the loo as the nerves were getting to me. Fenton was a popular race course and the place was filling up.

I was longer than expected as I bumped into several people I knew on the way. I had been gone for at least half an hour. When I got back to the stable there was no sign of Jenny but I saw the back of a person wearing a hoody rushing away. Raven was at the back of the stable snorting and sweating. He saw me, lurched forward, ears back and teeth bared.

"Hey, Raven, it's me, what's happened?"

The poor horses walked round and round the small stable clearly very distressed. He started to kick his belly and I feared he was coming down with colic. Jenny came running round the corner looking startled.

"Where the hell have you been? I told you not to leave him? Look at the state of him!"

I was furious.

"I had a call to go and help Don with Dance. I was only gone fifteen minutes."

Jenny was near to tears at the sight of Raven. I wasn't listening to her reply. I was talking in a soothing voice to try and calm him down. Eventually, I was able to put the head collar on him. I took him out of the stable walking around to try and prevent him from going down to roll as this would cause a twisted gut. Raven was snorting and frothing at the mouth. I thought he might have eaten something bad. I managed to get my hand in his mouth and grab his tongue. A large white stone fell out. Jenny picked up the stone.

"Someone must have tried to drug him with this. It's chalk with a hole in the middle for the drug."

"Oh no, who would do this?"

I pulled out my phone to ring Rob.

I was relieved to see Rob appear as I was walking Raven up and down the stable block.

"What's going on? How's he got in this state?"

Jenny and I told Rob what had happened.

Rob was angry at the near hysterical Jenny. She showed him the piece of chalk.

"Who would want to do this to him?" I asked Rob.

"There are always enemies in racing."

Rob shook his head and rubbed Raven on the neck.

"I'll get the vet to look at him but I don't think he'll be racing today."

I had already realised that, and although I was bitterly disappointed, I was more concerned that Raven would be OK.

The vet came quickly. He diagnosed colic and took a blood test to see if he had drugs in his system.

"I'll just give him a mild sedative to relax his muscles. When he's calmed down, you can take him home."

"Thanks a lot, Tim. You have got to him quickly before the damage was too bad."

Rob was grateful for the vet's prompt arrival.

Once they had cooled him down and he had shown no more signs of colic, Rob loaded Raven up into the lorry and they went back to the yard. Jenny and I monitored him all through the night. He was calm and sleepy from the sedative. Rob reported the case to the police and the racing authorities at Wetherby's, the racehorse headquarters. The incident was in the Racing Post warning people to be extra vigilant with their horses. Rob had no idea who could have done this to Raven. He decided that I should take him to the other side of the country for his first race.

Three months later we were on the road to Yorkshire. We would have to stay overnight to get over the journey. I was excited about the forthcoming adventure but also very nervous. I planned to sleep at the stables with Raven. Jenny was going with them and vowed not to take her eyes off him. It had taken hours of my time and patience with natural horsemanship to bring Raven back to the horse he was before the drugging incident.

I was very impressed with the facilities when I arrived at the yard. They had CCTV in every stable so that I was able to get something to eat and drink whilst watching Raven. There were bunk beds next to the tea room again with the CCTV. The friendly yard staff were horrified to hear what had happened to Raven at Fenton.

Everyone felt refreshed on the morning of the races as they got Raven ready for the race course. They arrived in good time for the second race. The horse was excited about the atmosphere and seemed to have forgotten his previous experience. Jenny was able to plait him up and made his coat gleam. She was thrilled when he won best turned out. All too soon I was riding down to the start.

"This is it, lad. Just do your best. That's all I ask," I spoke softly to him as much to calm my nerves as his.

I was relieved that this was one of the few racecourses left with no stalls at the start as Raven panicked in tight spaces. I could empathise with him as I was claustrophobic myself. Most likely traumatised after being put in the crate for the long journey on the ship to England. There were fourteen horses in the race which was a lot. I decided not to be too competitive and I wanted Raven's first race to be incident free.

The flags went up.

"We're off!" I shouted with excitement.

I kept to the outside track where I managed to avoid the mud splattering his face. The going was soft after last night's rain; luckily, the best condition for Raven. I felt the power surge up from his hind quarters as he leapt forward overtaking the field.

"Two furlongs to go and we're in third place!"

I showed Raven the stick as I urged him on even faster.

"Come on, my beauty, we can do it!"

184

Ears pricked, Raven seemed to find another gear when he heard my voice. We were in the lead. The crowd went mad as we sailed past them to the finish.

"We have won!"

I flung my arms round Raven's neck. I couldn't believe it.

"Well done, you, beauty."

Jenny was beside him with tears of happiness rolling down her face. Rob was there to greet them at the winner's enclosure.

"Well done, lad, that was an amazing performance."

"I couldn't believe the power in him, Rob, he's a born winner."

I was laughing and crying at the same time. Raven looked very proud of himself as the sash was put around him. All signs of fear had disappeared.

Chapter 28

Hattie

Hattie was shocked to hear of Fado's horse being drugged. She had heard that bad things happened in the racing world. Recently, she had read books about famous race horses and their journey to the top. Poor Fado had spent hours working with the horse; it was a cruel world. She despised anyone who could harm an animal. She spoke to him on the phone.

"Hi, Fado, how are things at the yard now?"

"Oh, Hattie, it's been terrible for poor Raven. I've had to spend hours trying to gain his trust again."

"You will have a lot to do to repair the damage that evil person did to him. Any clues about who it could have been?"

"No, I'm afraid not."

Fado was clearly distraught about the drugging incident. He was the sort of person who trusted everyone.

"Well not to worry, he'll be caught. What's your next plan with Raven?"

"We are going to take him out up north somewhere."

"Good idea. Best of luck with that."

Hattie was very proud of Fado. He had a natural talent with horses and showed wisdom and patience beyond his years around them.

"It would be great if you could come and watch us."

Hattie sensed that Fado was nervous about taking Raven to another race and needed her support.

"Of course, I will, Fado, just let me know the details."

Unfortunately, when it came to the week before the race, Sheila became ill. She had a fever and chest infection and she was struggling into work in the mornings. Hattie told her to go home for the afternoons, leaving her to get the ponies ready for their lessons. She had to tell Fado that she wasn't going to make it up to Yorkshire. His race fell on the busiest lesson day.

Fado was very disappointed and sounded near to tears when she told him.

"Oh, I'm so sorry, darling. But listen, you are going to be a winner. Just take deep breaths and focus on nothing else but the track in front of you. Do not let anyone distract you."

"OK, but I am so nervous and it's really stressful after what happened last time."

Hattie was near to tears herself as she felt so helpless unable to help her poor boy when she was at the end of the phone.

"I know, love, and it's understandable for you to feel that way. But remember what we always say, tomorrow's another day. What happened yesterday is in the past. Focus on the future. You are a winner, my boy."

Hattie didn't believe for a moment that Fado would win the race. He did not have the experience of the other jockeys and the horse was an unknown quantity. However, she needed him to have confidence and believe in himself.

"Thanks, Hattie. Will you be able to watch me on the TV?"

"I will do my best, love."

Hattie knew she would be busy at the stables at the three o'clock race time but she could watch it on catch up and ring Fado as soon as she had seen it.

She was in the middle of tacking up when her phone rang.

"Ahhhh! Did you see me? I won, can you believe it? Raven and I won! Did you see us, Hattie?"

"What? You actually won the race? My boy, I told you didn't I? I said you were a winner. Well done. I'll ring you as soon as I have watched it."

Hattie was thrilled for her beloved Fado. She told all the kids at the yard and they cheered. As soon as lessons had finished and the ponies were put away, she went to fetch her laptop. The people at the yard all gathered around in the tea room to watch it. It was a brilliant race. Fado rode so well, bringing Raven up to the front at just the right time so that he had the energy to push to the front.

Hattie rang Fado as everyone cheered their congratulations to him.

"Well done, you rode brilliantly."

"Thanks, Hattie. I did all the things you told me to and Raven did the rest. He is a top horse, a real winner."

"I can see that, but where would he have been without all your care and patience?"

"Probably in a can of dog food!"

Hattie told Fado to have a good time celebrating and she would look forward to seeing him at the weekend.

Chapter 29

Fado

I was surprised at the welcome I got when I arrived back at the yard. Other jockeys won races all the time and just got a pat on the back. I jumped out of the lorry to find everyone lined up clapping and cheering.

Rob called a meeting with me in the house.

"You and Raven were brilliant and really working together as a team to win that race."

"Thanks, Rob. I loved every minute of it."

"As for your immediate future together, you two need to get out every week If we're going to enter him in The Derby."

"OK, well, I'll have a look at the schedule and put a programme together to show you."

I could hardly believe that I was in training for the Derby. It was my ambition to be placed in the Derby and win enough money to go to Kenya and find my family. They were no nearer finding out who tried to drug Raven. After his win, they could see that he had real talent and someone from his past knew this. I had a feeling right from the start that he had been very badly treated because of his behaviour.

Rob told Fado that they would take extra staff to watch over him at the races and that he must not be left for a second. They had CCTV at the yard.

"I'm going to make enquiries throughout the industry to get to the bottom of this," Rob assured me.

I knew that Rob was highly respected in the racing world and if anyone could find out about Raven's past it would be him.

The next race was nearer to home so they did not need to stay overnight. I was going to be riding Starr and Raven. Jenny and Fee were going to watch over Raven whilst I was with Starr.

I was in the second race with Starr and the fifth with Raven. The girls were nervous as they watched over Raven. It was a big responsibility and they were suspicious of anyone who approached them. They stood either side of him protectively.

He was munching his hay oblivious of the worry he was causing. It was a relief when I gave the all clear to lead him around.

I was feeling great after coming third on Starr in a highly competitive race. I would be very happy if I could do the same or better on Raven.

The horse was on his toes as I went for a leg up. He seemed to have seen something that upset him. His head was high and he was snorting and jogging. It took three attempts for me to get on him.

"Find Rob and tell him that something or someone has upset Raven out here!" I instructed Jenny.

"OK, he's been fine in the stable."

Jenny couldn't understand Raven's sudden change of mood.

I tried to calm him with his soothing voice as they bucked and sidled their way down to the start. I was relieved there were no stalls again. In this mood they would never have got him in them. He was jigging about at the start and gave a huge double barrel kick as the flag went down. This delayed his start making it difficult for me to get in a good position being so far back. We stayed at the back wondering how to get around the closed bunch of horses ahead. I was horrified to witness a terrible incident. One of the jockeys in the middle raised his whip which caught the horse next to him in the eye. The poor horse reared over backwards landing onto the horse behind him. Within seconds there was a pile of horses and jockeys on the ground.

Being so far behind, we managed to skirt around them all and catch up with the leaders. As we went up the hill we lost pace.

"Come on, lad, don't give up now, we can do it."

I felt the power from behind as Raven surged forward and past them all to take the lead where we remained as we sailed over the finish.

The crowd were euphoric after such an exciting race. They loved Raven, who again, was by no means the favourite with the bookies. I was very happy but also concerned about the accident. I was determined to report what I had seen. Luckily, all the horses had got up and were not injured but one of the jockeys had a broken collar bone.

A steward's inquiry followed and the jockey who had used the whip was banned for twelve months. I had made sure that my report remained anonymous. I didn't want any more trouble for myself or Raven.

Rob decided not to declare Raven until his next race and on that day he would put him in as a late entry to see if he got spooked by anything, anybody or if no one knew he was racing.

The day before they were due to leave for a race in Dorset, Rob called me into his office.

"Come and look at this, lad, I think we have our man."

I leant over Rob to look on the computer. Rob had looked up racing accidents in the last few years.

There were many to look at but one had caught Rob's eye. It showed a jockey struggling in the stalls with a rearing horse. As the gates opened, the reins got caught in the hinge and the jockey was squashed between the gate and the stall as the horse thrashed around trying to free himself. Suddenly, the bridle broke and the horse leapt forward leaving the jockey with his arm trapped. The report said that the jockey had lost his arm in the accident and never rode again. The horse looked remarkably like Raven but was named Starlings Delight.

"That would be Raven's enemy, alright."

I told Jenny and Fee about the report. Jenny said she had seen a man with one arm walking around the stables when she was helping Don with Dance. Fee said she had noticed a man with one arm staring at them when she was leading Raven around the collecting ring.

"It must have been the man that spooked our beautiful horse!"

I gave a little smile as I realised how fond the girls had become of the horse.

I told Rob what the girls had seen.

"The problem is; we have no proof of him doing anything to Raven."

Rob was frustrated that there seemed little they could do about the one-armed jockey who clearly wanted to take revenge on the horse.

"We could set some traps for him. Then we can make sure he is caught on the CCTV."

I desperately wanted to catch the man who was trying to hurt my beloved horse.

"Let's just get tomorrow over with and hope its incident free."

Rob wanted some time to think about how he would handle the situation.

The Dorset race was a great success with no problems. Raven not only won the race but was really calm the whole time.

"Well, that tactic worked but we can only put in late entries at the smaller, less well-known racecourses."

"OK, next race we set traps. We must make sure we can have a video at the stable all the time."

Rob told everyone to get their heads together and come up with some ideas.

Raven was entered for a big race in Chester. Plans were made to get there early. They would set up the cameras and make sure they were working OK before leaving him.

They settled Raven into his stable with some hay.

Making sure there was no one watching, they put an alarm button outside the stable door, covering it in mud. Jenny and Fado went and hid in a spare stable nearby. Within fifteen minutes they saw someone passing their stable and then the alarm button went off. Jenny and Fado leapt out of their stable to see a man with one arm running off in the other direction. They went to see if Raven was OK. He was standing at the back of the stable snorting. Rob was waiting for the man at the end of the row of stables.

"Not so fast there, you're not going anywhere until you tell me what you were doing at my horses stable."

Rob noticed he was holding a penknife.

"That horse ruined my life. He's vicious and dangerous."

The man did not try and deny what he was going to do.

"If you go anywhere near that horse again, I'll have you arrested."

Rob had called for his friend who was a policeman to join them. He appeared just in time.

"Give me that penknife. Leave the race course now and do not come near this horse again. I'll make sure you are banned from going to the races for a few years."

The policeman towered over the little man being six foot six and eighteen stone.

"OK, I'm going, but it will only be a matter of time before that jockey of yours is killed by your evil horse."

The little man walked off quickly after handing over the penknife. The policeman followed him just to make sure he left the racecourse.

"Well, that was a result."

I turned to Rob and gave him a high five.

"Is Raven going to be OK to race?"

Rob was concerned after seeing the penknife.

"Yes, he's fine, Jenny's tacking him up."

I was surprised at Raven's calm mood going down to the start. He seemed to know his enemy had gone. I found he lacked energy. It was as if he was emotionally drained. He managed to come third in the race.

"Perhaps, we should have withdrawn him," I told Jenny.

"I agree, we didn't realise how much seeing that horrible man took out of him."

Jenny was still upset at the thought of what the man was going to do with the penknife to the horse she had grown very fond of. They went home feeling despondent but relieved that Raven was OK and they would not have to worry about his enemy again.

It was getting increasingly difficult to find races that did not have stalls to start the race. I asked Rob if Raven could have a couple of weeks off racing so that he could work on de-sensitizing him with his fear of tight spaces. Rob was not happy at this suggestion. Raven was on a winning streak and he wanted this to continue. I pointed out that there would be far more opportunity to win money if they could get the horse into the stalls.

Having studied the video of Raven's accident in the stalls, I knew I had a difficult task ahead. I started with the simple issue of dealing with tight spaces. I set up a row of cones with some bunting attached in the corner of the school. I put on his training head collar with the long rope attached and walked ahead of him around the school. As we approached the cones Raven snorted and backed away. I stood still and let him sidle all around the area; eventually, he went to put his nose on a cone, snorted and backed away. I remained calm and still next to the cones. Eventually, he stood next to the cones without fear. I then began to walk in between the fence and the cones. At first, Raven planted his feet, refusing to follow me. With gentle persuasion, he was following me alongside the cones within fifteen minutes. I was pleased with the session.

The next project would be harder to create. I secured some palettes to the fence and the jump wings. I put a pole over the top. Again, it was not easy to persuade Raven to walk under the mock stall. It took some time before Raven would take a few steps towards the structure. At last, he decided it was safe to walk through. They practiced every day for a week.

"It's hardly the real thing," Rob commented when he came to watch Raven's progress.

"Have you got any better ideas then?"

I was slightly annoyed at Rob's reaction as I had worked so hard on the project.

"Yes, as a matter of fact, I do. I know a chap who bought a disused racecourse to train his horses on. I'll give him a ring."

The following week they spent the day at Rob's friend's racecourse.

"Come on lad, let's have a look at these stalls."

The horse would get so far, then snort and rear going backwards away from them. After numerous attempts, I managed to get him to stand with his front feet at the gate of the stalls. He planted his feet but without rearing and snorting. His head hung low in submission. At this point, I took Raven away for a break. I turned him out into a small paddock whilst I ate my packed lunch.

Rob's friend came over to me.

"You've got the patience of a saint there, lad."

"Well, there's no point in pushing it. He has to overcome his fear himself and in his own time. No good will come out of rushing him."

"You've got wisdom beyond your years', lad. That horse is lucky he found you."

"Thanks, I feel lucky to have the opportunity to work with him."

By the end of the day, just before the light began to fade, Raven finally decided it was OK to enter the stalls. He walked through them five or six times without any problem. I was exhausted as I led him up the ramp of the lorry. I was relieved to get home and very pleased with the results of the day.

Chapter 30
The Gold Cup

I took Raven to some races with stalls. After a bit of messing around he did eventually go in and stay calm in them. This progress gave us more opportunity to enter races with or without stalls.

This was a great help in the lead up to The Gold Cup. A couple of weeks before the big race we came second in a big race. I was very pleased with Raven as he showed me he could be up there with the lead horses. Winning the big race meant so much to me. Not only would I be nominated for 'Jockey of the year',the money would give me enough to go to Kenya and find my family. I had saved as much of my winnings as possible over the past couple of years. I wanted to give them my money so that they could make a better life for themselves.

Justin had been helping me to try and trace their whereabouts. We had discovered the estate that they had gone to after they had been moved out of Tristan's place. I had tried writing to the owner but had not had a reply. I knew that it would be difficult to gain information unless I actually went there. Sometimes, owners of the estates on the Mara spent a little time at the place. The servants would run the estate in their absence. If I won this race, I would have enough money for the trip and to help my family. I rang Hattie to see if she could go and watch me. I really valued her support. I would be grateful to her forever for all she had done for me. I had discussed my plans to go to Kenya with her and she was very supportive.

"Of course, I'm coming to watch you! In fact, I'm planning to stay in the hotel on the Downs. The girls are coming and maybe some people from the stables as well." Hattie also hoped that her son would join them as he lived close to the racecourse.

"Well, that's quite a party then. I hope Raven is on top form to show everyone his true colours."

I was very happy that Hattie seemed as excited as me about the race.

"I'll have to be very focussed though, Hattie. Please don't think I'm being anti-social if I don't talk to anyone before the race."

"Don't worry, I'll keep everyone entertained and we'll celebrate with you after the race."

"Thanks, Hattie. It means so much to me having you there."

I heard Hattie sniffling as she said goodbye. I knew she was going to miss me when I went to Kenya and I would miss her so much.

Hattie checked the horses and walked the dogs at the crack of dawn on the morning of the race. The sunrise was beautiful lighting up the sky in all shades of red and purple. The birds gave her their dawn chorus and she could smell the fresh scent of wild roses in the hedgerows. She stood watching her horses graze with the sea on the horizon behind them. It was times like this that she felt very lucky to be alive and live where she did. She put her arms around the big oak tree and leaning her cheek against the rough warm bark, she asked for help and guidance for Fado today.

Justin had a court case and couldn't go, so, he would stay and look after the dogs, goats and hens and a couple of the girls who were back from university would look after the yard.

They were off in good time and the journey was smooth with little traffic. There was already a great atmosphere at the racecourse when they arrived.

The fairground was buzzing. The gypsy campsite was very colourful with the men having trotting races on their little cobs. The women looked amazing in their flamboyant and dazzling dresses.

Hattie walked through the gypsy camp on her way to find Fado. She had left the others exploring the place with strict instructions not to let Fado see them.

"A moment of your time, my love?" an old lady with a tanned and lined face beckoned her.

Hattie had a fascination for these people and she couldn't help herself being drawn towards the woman.

"You are a good and kind lady. Your kindness must be rewarded. You must slow down; it's not good for you to do so much. Your health will suffer, my dear. Take more care. Today will change a lot for you."

The woman withdrew backwards into a tent as Hattie stood unable to move for a moment. A withered arm poked out of the tent with an old cloth hat upturned. Hattie realised that she should put some money in it for the woman's words of wisdom. She shoved a £5 note in the hat and hurried off telling herself that she should not have stopped to listen to the old gypsy. The old lady's words lay deep inside her. She knew her life was far too busy and that she had little time to think about herself but she didn't know how to change. Also changing her life was not really an option for her. How could the events of today change things for her? She hurried along to the stables trying to put the words out of her mind.

When I walked the course with Rob I found it was like no other I had ridden before. It was steep in places and there were sharp corners. It was like riding a cross-country course. Rob had given his advice on how to ride the difficult parts, particularly the famous Tottenham corner.

"You need to steady up and try to keep to the outside. If you go too fast on the downhill approach you will get off balance on the corner."

I could see that this was sound advice.

"Well, I can try, but slowing down on that downhill stretch may be easier said than done."

Hattie's arrival was a welcome distraction.

"Hi, Hattie, I need a hug to calm my nerves. I've just walked the course with Rob."

"Come here, darling. You are the best of jockeys, you'll be fine."

I was as always comforted by Hattie's words.

"I need to go and have another look at Tottenham corner. Will you come with me?"

"Come on, let's go, and put your mind at rest."

Hattie linked arms with him as they strode off to the course together. Rob watched them with a smile. He was relieved to see Hattie calming the boy down. There was no denying it was a very big challenge for him and the horse. The one-armed man's words rang in his ears, 'That horse is vicious, it's only a matter of time, he'll be the death of the boy.'

Rob would never forgive himself if anything happened to that boy.

As we walked the course, I told Hattie how I had trained Raven to go into the stalls.

"He's such a brave horse to overcome all his fears and win races."

"You have done a marvellous job with him and it's because you believe in him that he does so well."

"I am really nervous about this race, Hattie. The course is the longest and most undulating that I have ever ridden."

"I can see that, love, but you two are as one and will ride it well."

"I want this so much! If I win, I can go to Kenya and help my family."

"It's that goal that will get you around, just do your very best and keep focussed."

Hattie was really pleased that they had the chance to have a heartfelt chat. She was very touched that Fado wanted to find his family and help them. A part of her was worried that he may stay in Kenya and she would lose him forever. She pushed these thoughts to the back of her mind. Fado must find his family and help them. She was proud that he wanted to.

When they got back, I went off to get ready for the race and giving me a kiss and a hug, Hattie went off to find her crowd. She found them in the grandstand. They had got there early to get a good position. Everyone wanted to know how Fado was feeling. Hattie told them how she had walked the course to Tottenham corner and admitted she could see why he was worried about it. Hattie left them so that she could go and watch Raven in the collecting ring and see Fado safely mounted. She recognised Jenny leading the horse around and gave a little wave. She looked as nervous as Fado. Raven held his head high alert to his surroundings and his coat was glistening in the sunshine. Fado came into the ring and spotting her straight away, he gave her a broad smile. Hattie was reassured that he was feeling strong. Raven whickered when he saw Fado who gave him a rub before getting a leg up. Hattie went back to the stand where the others were cheering as Raven and Fado jogged down to the start.

Hattie's heart was thumping as the flag went down and they were off. Fado had managed to position himself on the outside of the long line of horses.

The atmosphere was electric as the horses galloped past the grandstand. Everyone was cheering and shouting for the horse that they had backed. Hattie caught a glimpse of Fado, head down and totally focussed as he flew past on Raven. They watched the screen as the close-knit bunch of horses approached Tottenham corner. Hattie could not see how the middle group were going to cope with the corner at the great speed they were going. Surely, the ones nearest to the fence would be pushed into it on the tight corner. Fado stuck to the outside as they raced down the hill. He was not with the leading horses.

******

As we raced down towards the tight corner, I could see that the four horses in the middle were going too fast.

"Steady up now, lad, we need to slow down here."

I squeezed my hands around the reins and could see Raven's ears twitching as he listened to me and slowed down. Suddenly, the four horses in the middle were crashing into each other and the inside rider hit the fence. The jockey went flying over it and the loose horse's stirrup flew off, hitting the middle horse. He bucked throwing his jockey off.

"It's OK, steady up now, lad!" I shouted into Raven's ears more out of fear at the horror I was witnessing.

I knew we just had to ride on and keep focussed. Remaining on the outside, we managed to escape the carnage going on. Raven found his top gear as he could see the clear run to the finish and shot to the front. The crowd went mad as we sailed past them to win the race.

"Raven's beauty ridden by Fado Favier, trained by Rob Robertson and owned by John Watson has won the Gold Cup." The commentator could hardly be heard over the screams and cheers of the crowd.

As we rode into the winner's enclosure, tears of joy streamed down my face and I couldn't believe that all my friends and family were there to greet me. Jenny was throwing her arms round Raven's neck. Rob was patting my leg shouting,

"Well done, lad, well ridden, I am so proud of you."

A microphone was thrust at me.

"How does it feel to win the Gold cup?" the TV commentator asked.

"It's hard to take in at the moment, but I'm so proud of this one," I told him patting Raven.

I actually thought I must be dreaming; my dream had finally come true. The hard work had paid off. I had achieved my ultimate goal.

Raven was washed down and walked round to cool off and I was presented with the Gold Cup in front of hundreds of flashing cameras and my family and friends were shouting, "Hooray! Well done, Fado."

The press was all around me.

"Were you born in England?" one newspaper reporter asked.

"No, I'm from Kenya," I replied.

"How long have you lived here?"

"Since, I was nine."

"Did you move here with your parents?"

"No, I came on the Napoli."

Rob grabbed my arm and waved the press away.

"That's enough of your interrogating. The boy has won the Gold Cup. He's a famous jockey now."

Hattie, in floods of tears, ran to the entrance of the enclosure and planted a huge kiss on my cheek.

"My, darling boy, you did it. You were brilliant, every inch of the race."

"Aw, thanks, Hattie, Raven is the most amazing horse."

I went over to give him some Polo mints. Raven nuzzled him gratefully.

When they had settled him back into his stable cooling him down by rubbing straw all over him and wrapping him in a fleece, I gave him electrolytes to replace the salt and minerals he had lost through sweating. Jenny assured him she would stay with Raven and encouraged him to go and celebrate with his family and friends. They ate and drank late into the night, all so happy and excited.

The family woke up the next morning to find their faces on every newspaper.

'Shipwrecked boy wins the Gold Cup. The family who rescued him are very proud.'

'Castaway Wins the Gold Cup.'

'Poor boy from Kenya rises to fame as a jockey.'

'From Stowaway to Famous Jockey.'

"Where did the press get all this information from?"

Hattie was furious that the wonderful events of yesterday had turned into a newspaper scandal. She rang Justin to ask his advice. He told her it was typical of the press. They would probably be waiting outside the hotel to pounce on them and bombard them with more questions. He advised them to say nothing, use the fire exits to reach their cars and avoid the press.

"How did they find out all about Fado?"

"That's what the press does, Hattie. If you say one word, they will make it into ten."

"Oh Lord, what have we got ourselves into?"

"Don't worry, love, today's news is history tomorrow."

"OK, well, I'll warn everyone not to say anything else to them."

The whole family felt like burglars as they crept down the fire escape and ran to their cars. As they drove away, the press was running after them shouting questions.

Hattie was relieved to be back at the farm and out of the public eye. Everyone at the stables was very excited at the wonderful news. Justin had a lovely dinner prepared for her. She was very happy to see him.

The next morning Fado phoned Hattie.

"Hattie, you'll never guess what, 'This Morning' have phoned me, they want me to go on their programme."

"Oh my, you are really going to be famous."

"I know, well, so are you. They will want to know all about you."

"Now, you be careful what you say."

"Ha! Don't worry I will."

Chapter 31

Fado

I woke up feeling really nervous about my television interview. I phoned home and Justin answered.

"Just be yourself. You'll be fine talking about your passion which comes naturally to you."

"Thanks, Justin, you're right, I feel better now."

Once I had met the presenters, I was fine and they made me feel at ease. I was soon telling them my life story forgetting about all the cameras in my face.

"Have you thought of writing a book?" Sue asked him.

"I'm afraid, English was never my best subject at school."

"Well, your story would make a very good read, it's fascinating."

"Ha, I know it is an unusual story. Even if I did have the ability, I wouldn't have the time."

"What are you going to do next, now that you have won The Gold Cup?"

"I'm taking a break from racing to travel to Kenya. I want to find my family and use the money I have earned to help them."

I hadn't really talked about this to anyone before. I surprised myself announcing my intentions on television. Hattie will be upset that we haven't really discussed this.

"Can you tell us about your family, Fado?"

I wanted to change the subject or better yet, end the interview.

"I don't really know much about them as I was only nine when I was put in the boat." I said quietly feeling subdued.

"Well, you really are an inspiration to us all with your achievements. Thank you very much for your time today. It's been a pleasure to meet you."

I was relieved to be leaving the studio. I was dreading the inevitable phone call from Hattie.

The phone rang just as I was going into the train station.

"Hi, darling. Well done, we all thought you were brilliant."

I could detect the hesitation in Hattie's voice.

"Oh good. It was a bit nerve wracking but I really enjoyed it."

"Great, well, I must dash, but we'll have a chat this evening, I'll ring you at seven."

"OK, speak later."

I knew what that conversation would be about. I'd have to think about what to say about my plans to go to Kenya. I had mentioned my wish to find my family a few times. It had always been on my mind but I hadn't actually told Hattie when I would go. Actually, I surprised myself when answering the question during the interview. It suddenly dawned on me that now was the time to go whilst I had the money.

"Hi, Fado; at last, we have time for a proper chat and a catch up."

Hattie tried to sound chirpy taking the tension out of her voice.

"Yes, it's been quite a few hectic days since the race. How are you anyway?"

"Oh, I'm fine, busy as usual, you know how it is. Actually, I wanted to hear more about your plans, Fado!"

"Well, the thing is, I have always wanted to save up enough money to go to Kenya."

"Fado, I could have helped you; we could have gone together."

"I know that. But try and understand, this is something I really want to do on my own."

"OK, I'll try to see your point of view. I knew the day would come when you wanted to find your family. It's just that I always thought we would do this together."

"Hattie, you have done more than enough for me. Now, it's time for me to learn about my origins and be independent."

I heard Hattie sniff and clear her throat before she answered. I felt a tear come into my eyes at the thought of upsetting her.

"I promise you, that I'll call you every step of my journey. When I am reunited with my family, you'll be the first person to know."

"Of course, I will. I just hope that you'll be happy, that's all I want to know."

"I will be and I'll want you to come out to Kenya and meet my family."

"Oh, don't you worry about that, I'll be out like a shot as soon as I'm invited."

"That's all good then. I'll be home next week to arrange flights."

"OK, see you then, my love."

Hattie and I had talked about my family and one day going to find them. But I really wanted to go out to Kenya by myself even though I knew she was upset about this.

Having made my decision to go as soon as possible, the next thing to do was let Rob know.

"Hi, Rob, can I have a word?"

"Yes, lad, have you recovered from your stardom yet?"

"Ha! Ha! I have to tell you about a decision I've made."

"O–Oh I have a feeling I might not like it."

"Well, I have decided to go to Kenya and find my family."

"Ah yes, I thought you might want to do something like that. Of course, you can take a holiday, lad."

Rob sounded happy about me going on a holiday. But the trouble was I had no idea how long I would be away.

"The problem is Rob, I have no idea how long I'll want to be away for. I guess I should hand in my notice."

Rob frowned and shook his head.

"That's not a good idea. When you want to return, I can't guarantee a place here for you."

"I know that Rob. I wouldn't expect you to hold my place indefinitely. I just don't know whether I will find my family and if I do, what will I decide to do then."

"I'll tell you what I can do. Much as I'm very sad to see you go, I can see it's something you have to do. I'll hold your place here for a year. That way, you will have a job to come back to."

"Thanks, Rob, that's a very generous offer and I'd like to accept it."

"You're a good lad and very talented, I'd be very sorry to see you go."

I felt better having got the two difficult conversations out of the way. I decided to go and ask the girls if they'd like to go for a drink. I told Jenny I was leaving.

"Oh, Fado, I'll miss you so much."

She flung her arms around me.

"So, will the horses."

The other girls joined in a group hug.

Chapter 32

Justin

Justin tried to comfort Hattie who he had never seen so down. She was near to tears every evening. They both agreed that it was the right thing for Fado to do.

"Life just won't be the same without Fado popping home in between races." Hattie spoke with tears in her eyes.

"I know; I'll miss him as well."

Justin suppressed a smile as he thought of Fado crashing through the door leaping around as he talked twenty to the dozen about his latest antics at the racing yard.

"He lights up the room with his endless energy and positive attitude," Justin reassured Hattie that whatever happened, Fado would always stay in touch with her and would never forget all that she had done for him.

"He said he would like me to go out there when he is reunited with his family."

Hattie was trying to look on the positive side.

"Well, there you are then, something to look forward to."

Justin put his arm around Hattie relieved to see her brightening up.

Fado bounced into the farm house a week later full of enthusiasm and excitement about his trip. They spent the week shopping and gathering things together. Hattie realised how much she would miss his chatter, clutter and noise around the place. She had got used to him living away but always looked forward to his regular visits back home whenever he had a break from racing. Justin helped Fado to find a reasonably priced flight for the following month.

"You will keep us posted, won't you, Fado? Hattie is very upset that you are leaving, even though she understands and supports you in your decision."

"Of course, I will, Justin. I will never forget the wonderful life Hattie has given me and you will all remain close to my heart forever."

Justin gave Fado a hug holding back a tear as they completed the booking online for the flight.

His job now was to organise a good send off for the boy and keep strong for Hattie. He would suggest a family gathering and party. Arranging things would take Hattie's mind off the departure of her dear boy.

Chapter 33

Hattie

Hattie was rushed off her feet in the weeks leading up to Fado's departure. Everyone had accepted the invitation to a farewell party. Hattie spent any time she had, once all was done at the stables, making quiche, pies, buns, scones and cakes. It was a great help to be kept so busy and Hattie was grateful to Justin for suggesting the idea of giving Fado a good send off. Hattie wanted to get everything organised before Fado arrived home. Once he was back, she wanted to take him shopping to buy things for his family.

At last, the day arrived for Justin and Hattie to collect Fado from the racing yard. Rob greeted them and they were all invited for a cup of tea with his wife and the main jockeys. Rob presented Fado with a beautiful model racehorse.

"Wow, thanks, Rob, I shall treasure this forever. Thank you so much for having me here. I have learnt all I know about racing from you. I will be eternally grateful for all the opportunities you have given me."

"We have loved having you here. Our little project. You have done us proud."

Everyone clapped, hugged each other and shed a few tears. It was a moving departure from the life Fado had led for the past few years.

Back home Hattie and Fado made lists of things needed for the trip to Kenya. Hattie loved spending time alone with Fado and would cherish this precious time.

"It looks like we have got some shopping to do. You won't be wearing jodhpurs every day in Kenya and you don't seem to have much else to wear."

Hattie was shocked to see that Fado had very few clothes.

"Yes I know, but my wardrobe was not a priority in my life. No good having a load of clothes I never wear."

"Well, now your life is changing, you'll need a new wardrobe."

"OK, but I don't like shopping. Too stuffy in those big stores. Can we get everything in one shop?"

"I know what you mean; I'm not one for traipsing around different shops either. We should be able to get everything from the one big department store in town."

"Great, then we can treat ourselves to lunch."

Hattie realised she would have to set aside a day for the shopping trip but was sure Sheila wouldn't mind.

They had a very successful trip buying all they needed and had a good laugh together. Hattie sat down with Justin in the evening recalling the day's events.

"He has grown into such a good, kind and thoughtful person."

"Well, of course he has. You gave him the best groundwork he could have wished for."

Justin gave Hattie a hug.

"I am going to miss him so much."

Hattie couldn't help a tear rolling down her cheek.

"Hey now, cheer up, we've a party to host before he goes. How are his plans coming on?"

"Oh, everything is under control. He doesn't know exactly what's happening although he does suspect that something is."

"I can't wait to see his face when he sees everyone here."

They both smiled at the thought and Hattie went to bed with the plans for the party on her mind.

It was the day of the party and two days before Fado departed for Kenya. Justin took Fado out for some last-minute essentials whilst Hattie got the party ready. Sheila went in to help Hattie when she had finished at the stables.

Everyone arrived at the house whilst Justin kept Fado out taking him to the pub. Hattie was a good host offering food and drinks around with no time to feel sad about what the party was actually for.

"What are all these cars doing in the car park, Justin?"

"Hattie must be doing one of her demos."

"Funny, she didn't say anything about it."

"Oh well, you know what Hattie's like, full of surprises,"

Justin gave a chuckle as he put an arm on Fado's shoulder guiding him towards the house.

The door flung open and everyone was waiting in the hall with party poppers.

"Surprise!" everyone shouted.

"What are you all doing here?"

Fado threw his arms wide as if he wanted to hug everyone with tears in his eyes.

It was a brilliant sending off with everyone giving their memories of Fado's life at Hattie's. Fado loved the evening and told everyone he would treasure the memory and miss them all.

Chapter 34

Fado

It's the day of departure. I felt a mixture of excitement, sadness and anxiety. I am dreading the 'goodbyes'. Also, I am nervous about flying. I don't like the thought of travelling alone. I'm not going to share this fear with anyone. Hattie will try and get me a chaperone like little kids have. I'll have to keep my worries to myself.

"Have you got your passport?" Justin asked.

"Yes, here it is, I'll put it in my bum bag."

"Good idea, right, I'll get this case into the car, you bring the rest."

"OK, come on, Hattie, we're loading the car."

"Coming, love. Just sorting the dogs out before we go."

Hattie appeared with a red face. She hadn't been able to stop crying whilst walking the dogs. I put my arm round her.

"Give me your phone. I'll show you how to FaceTime and Skype."

"Oh dear, I'm not good with all this modern technology."

"It's easy; look, just press this button and you'll be able to see my ugly face whilst you're talking to me."

"I will look forward to that. I'm sure I can get the girls at the stables to help me if I get stuck."

"Come on then, let's be on our way," Justin called from the car.

At the airport I thought it best to get through to the departure lounge and not prolong the sad farewells. I turned back to give a final wave to see tears rolling down Hattie's rosy cheeks. I felt choked and suddenly very alone. I found it hard to cope with the security checks as tears were misting up my eyes.

"Here you are love, don't forget your belt. Don't want your trousers falling down, do we?"

A tall smartly dressed middle-aged lady was handing me my belt.

"Oh thanks, it's easy to lose things."

I was grateful for the kind lady's help.

"It is when you have to put so much through security now. Where are you travelling to?"

"I'm going to Kenya to find my family."

"Well that's a coincidence. I'm going to Kenya as well. I'm a journalist doing some research on wildebeest in the Mara."

"No! Well, that's where I'm heading."

"Looks like we've got ourselves a travelling partner then. Pleased to meet you; I'm Sebrina."

The attractive journalist held out her hand for me to shake.

"Fado, I have to admit I'm relieved to meet you. I'm a bit nervous about flying and was not looking forward to travelling alone."

"I have to travel alone all the time but find it really boring being a journalist with a passion for any good story. I usually latch onto anyone who looks interesting."

"I expect you'll find me an unusual case then, I'm off to find something to eat now, I was too nervous to eat breakfast, I'm starving."

"Me too, I was up too early for breakfast."

I was really pleased to have found Sebrina. We seemed to hit it off right from the start. I felt less worried being with a regular traveller.

The time flew and we were boarding. Sebrina made notes as I told her my story.

"I don't want to forget any detail. This would make a good book! I've always wanted to write one."

"People have always told me to write a book about my life. I struggle with English so it would not be possible."

"You tell your story so well with your beautiful language. If you ever do decide to write about it I could help you. But now, you'll have a whole lot more to tell when you find your family. This is a new chapter."

"Life is a journey and the trouble with writing about your own life is that the journey is never over."

"You're right there. Shall we choose a film to watch?"

We watched The Lion King deciding it would get us in the mood for the country we were about to land in. Sebrina told me that she was going to look into her family history as well whilst she was away. Her great grandmother was born in Nairobi and her great grandfather on her father's side was brought up in the Caribbean.

When we landed in Nairobi, Sebrina and I went to the bus station to find out about buses out to The Maasi Mara. We got on a bus which would take three hours to the outskirts. We would have to get a jeep to Delamere. Sebrina had been in contact with the people who owned the estate and they had a tourist business. They had agreed to her filming and reporting on the wildebeest. I knew that my family had been employed by the previous owners of this place and hoped I would get some information about them from anyone still working there.

When we arrived at Delamer, Sebrina and I parted company as she was going up to the big house whilst I was going into the village. We had already exchanged phone numbers and email addresses promising to keep in touch.

The village consisted of a sea of mud huts. Brightly coloured clothes hung in between them on pieces of string. Smoke came out of the thatched roves of each hut. Some had cooking pots on the fires outside them and women with their little children gathered around occasionally stirring the contents of the pot.

Cows wandered freely about with bells around their necks. Little boys with sticks were herding groups of goats through the village towards the vast open space of Mara. Women were coming into it carrying big pots of water on their heads.

I wandered around fascinated by the village life. Flashbacks of my childhood were coming into my mind.

"Hey, mister."

A cheeky faced little boy of about nine years old was tugging at my shirt with his friends giggling behind him.

"Hello, my name is Fado, what's yours?"

"Charlie!" the little boy shouted with all of his friends laughing out loud.

"Well, Charlie, can you take me to your father?"

Charlie took hold of my shirt sleeve and pulled me along to a corral. A very tall man dressed in a bright red, orange and yellow cloth was tapping the cows with a long stick as if to sort them into groups.

"Papa! I find a man," Charlie called to his father.

The man looked up and beckoned his son to come into the corral. Charlie climbed over the fence to join his father. To my horror, his father got hold of a cow, cut its neck with a knife and caught the blood that was spilling out in a pouch. He then gave the blood to Charlie to drink. He stopped the bleeding with a piece of rag and sent the cow on its way. Charlie turned to me and gave me a blood-stained grin.

"Now, he the strongest boy," declared Charlie's father.

I could only nod in agreement completely lost for words at the ritual I had just witnessed. I tried to recall if my father had performed the same on me but couldn't remember.

Charlie brought his father over to me.

"I'm Fado."

I extended my hand to shake his.

"I have travelled from England to try and find my family."

Charlie repeated what I had said to his father in his own language.

"Welcome, come to my hut and have a drink."

I followed Charlie and his father to a hut.

The woman stopped stirring the pot and went to fetch a large jug and some cups. She gave us a drink of sweet red punch. It tasted good. She called Charlie another name. It turned out that Charlie had learnt the English names from tourists. He was a very bright boy and also learnt how to speak English from them.

I told my story with Charlie's help. His father told his son to tell me that he did remember the man who was killed by a hippo whilst saving a tourist's life. He remembered that the family had left the village and thought they had gone to work on the next estate.

"Charlie, how can I get to the next village?"

"Come this way, I show you."

Charlie asked his father if he could escort me to the next village.

Luckily for me, his father agreed and we were on our way to the donkey corral. Charlie found us a couple of ass to ride on. His mother ran after us with water carriers and some rice cakes.

"How long will it take us to get there?" I asked Charlie.

"About two days," Charlie answered casually as if this wasn't too bad.

I was worried about how we could sleep out in the wild and what about the lions?

"It's OK. I have a rifle. We sleep in a hut, no worries."

I was slightly reassured as we set off on our journey. We saw giraffes, elephants, zebras, wildebeest and Impala. I felt at home and memories of my childhood came flooding back.

"Big cats are sleeping now, they wake up at night when we are in the hut."

"That's OK then, I hope we find the hut in time."

"Mr Fado, you worry too much," laughed Charlie.

Sure enough, we arrived at a hut at dusk and Charlie said we must light a fire to frighten the lions.

Surprisingly, I did get a few hours of sleep. We were up at dawn and on our way after having some rice cakes and water.

We arrived at the village before dusk and Charlie took me to meet the chief man. I told my story again.

The chief nodded and told Charlie he thought that my mother, brother and sisters were all working on the estate.

"This is good news, Mr Fado. We wait here; your family will be back soon."

"I can't believe it. My whole family are still here!"

Tears came into my eyes at the thought of seeing them again.

"Come on; we go and wait for them."

I was feeling really anxious.

"I'm not sure how I will recognise my family," I confessed.

"No worries, Mr Fado, a mother never forgets her son."

"Charlie, I haven't seen any of them since I was nine years old."

"OK, I will ask people to tell us who they are when they all come back."

I was so relieved to have this wise and helpful little boy at my side.

The villagers returned in groups, chattering to each other along the path.

Chapter 35

All the villagers returning from their day's work in the fields or at the big house looked very tired. They walked with heads down and took slow steps.

I really didn't know how I would be able to recognise my family. But Charlie was right; my mother looked up as she walked past me.

"FADO!" she called stopping dead in her tracks and holding out her arms to me.

"Oh, Mum, is it really you?"

I fell into her arms and tears streamed down my face.

Charlie was jumping up and down in excitement sharing our joy.

"Favier, Jobo, Redir, this is your brother," my mother called her children over to me.

We all hugged and kissed for what seemed like a long time before Charlie led us to the centre of the village. People were congregating around the fire; some were having a drink and some were sharing soup from the big pot over the fire. Charlie announced to everyone that I had come all the way from England to be with my family.

Everyone came and hugged me. It was an overwhelming welcome into the heart of these wonderful people.

A chair was brought out for me to sit on. The women went to their huts gathering food and drink. Everyone sat down around me. They wanted to hear my story. My mother sat on a chair beside me. Her beautiful and warm smile made me so happy to be home.

I spent the next few days with my brothers working in the fields whilst my mother and sister worked at the big house. The work was very hard; cutting the crops with scythes and no machinery in the burning heat. After the day's work, everyone ate together around the communal fire. They didn't complain about their lives; they didn't have any luxuries but they wanted nothing.

"Mum, what would you like to do with your life if you didn't work at the big house?" I asked one evening.

Everyone stopped their chatter to listen to my mother's answer.

"I love sewing. I would make beautiful clothes for everyone."

Some of the villagers stood up holding out their dresses and giving a twirl.

"Did you make all their clothes?" I asked smiling at them in approval.

"Yes I did; when the evenings are light, I make clothes."

My mother didn't seem to realise how talented she was.

"Jobo, if you didn't work the fields every day, what would you like to do?"

"I would like to make things with wood," he answered. "Some of the children ran up to me with beautifully carved toys."

"Did you make these toys?" I asked my eldest brother.

"Yes; I also made all the furniture in our hut," he replied.

227

I went to my hammock that night full of ideas. I had to work out how to persuade my family to leave the village so that I could help them to start their own businesses in the city.

I did not go to the fields to work with them the next day. I spent the day finding a spot where I got a signal with my phone. I needed to get some advice from Justin and hadn't spoken to Hattie for ages.

"Hello, Hattie, how are you?"

"Hello, stranger! I'm fine, missing you lots; tell me your news."

"Well, I've been spending lots of time with my family getting to know them. I've even been going to work the fields with my brothers."

There was so much to tell Hattie about my new life.

"Oh, that sounds like hard work and very different from your life here."

Hattie sounded a bit down.

"Not really; you know all about hard work with the horses, but it is very hot. Are you OK? You sound tired."

I was concerned and felt a little guilty that I hadn't been in touch before.

"Yes, I'm fine; just tired with all the work. I'm thinking of finding a new teacher to help me out a bit," Hattie told me.

"That sounds like a very good idea. You need to ease your workload. I need some advice from Justin; is he around?"

"Yes, he's just on the tractor bringing hay around; I'll call him."

Hattie shouted for Justin.

"Hi, Fado, lovely to hear from you."

Justin sounded as jolly as ever.

"I'm fine, I need your advice. I want to get my family away from this estate. I would like them to go to the city and start their own business. I knew what I wanted to do but didn't know how to go on about it."

"OK, what sort of business?"

Justin wanted to know the answer.

"A dressmaker for my mother and a carpenter for my brother."

"That sounds great. You need to go to the estate owner and tell him you're leaving. Go to the bank in Nairobi and ask them to help you but you will need to take a business plan to show them. I'll put something together for you and send it by email."

Justin sounded very enthusiastic about the idea.

"Thanks, Justin, I'll make an appointment with the estate owner and the bank."

"Good luck lad, keep in touch."

Justin handed the phone back to Hattie.

"From what I could gather listening to that conversation, you have good plans for your family, Fado."

Hattie sounded brighter.

"Yes, Hattie, lots of exciting plans. I'll keep you posted."

"Look forward to hearing from you soon, love."

"Bye, Hattie, take care."

I called the family to my mother's hut when they returned from work. We discussed all the plans for their future. My mother was apprehensive as she had never known any other life but this. She was also a little scared of her boss. I assured her that we would all go and see him and I would do the talking. We planned to go and see him at the end of the week.

Chapter 36

The meeting with the big boss was not exactly pleasant. We all stood in the vast hall and we weren't invited any further into the house. I did the talking.

"If you are all insisting on leaving together, then you won't be getting this month's wages and I'll expect you gone by Friday week," the boss growled at us.

I put my arm around my mother who looked very frightened.

"Yes, sir, I hope that you can understand. I want to give my family a better life," I told him as I turned to leave.

The boss opened the door and ushered us out.

"Well, I'm glad that's over! What a horrible man."

"Fado, you can't be so disrespectful, he's our boss man," my mother scolded me as we all hurried away from the big house.

We spent the week preparing to leave as well as working. At last, we were ready to leave early on Saturday morning. All the villagers helped us to load up the wagon. Everyone was in tears as they hugged and kissed us. My mother was so upset that I wondered if I had done the right thing. She had never known any other life and the whole village were like a family to her. My brothers and sister comforted her. They were all excited about their new adventure.

The meeting with the bank manager went well. He was really helpful as he knew of properties we could buy. We found a house on the outskirts of the town. It had a bit of land with it so that we could have some chickens, goats and also grow our own vegetables. My mother was really happy about this as she would have found it very difficult to live in the town. Also, the house had a basement which we could make into her space for dressmaking. My sister could care for the animals after school.

The sheds outside would be workshops for both my brothers' carpentry business. There was also enough land for me to have a couple of horses. If I needed more, there was land surrounding this place that I could rent. I had plans to do something with horses but would start my family off in their work first.

We rented a house in town. Whilst the house sale was going through, my mother got a job at the local dressmakers. My brothers helped out at a builder's yard. My sister loved going to school every day.

Once we got the keys to our house all our spare time was spent making alterations. My brothers converted the outer buildings into a workshop for their carpentry. My mother, sister and I decorated the interior and got the basement ready for her dressmaking business.

It was easier to contact Hattie when we were in the city. I rang every week with news of our plans.

"You are getting on so well, Fado."

Hattie was always enthusiastic about my latest updates.

"When my family are established in their new businesses, I want to do something with horses."

I wanted to reassure Hattie that I hadn't lost interest in my passion.

"I certainly hope you will. I would love to come out and help you to buy some horses."

"Oh, Hattie, I would love you to."

I was genuinely delighted by this suggestion.

"What about September? The horses would still be living out and I could ask Sheila if she could stay at the house."

"Great, that gives us a few months to get ourselves sorted here."

"I shall really look forward to it."

I was so happy that Hattie could come and visit us. I ran to tell my mother the good news.

******

It was a very important day for me collecting Hattie from the airport and introducing her to my family. They all got on very well. Hattie and I had a lovely time travelling around and trying horses out. We chose a beautiful thoroughbred mare and a couple of ponies. My idea was to find a good stallion to breed from. I wanted to breed and bring on my own racehorses. Hattie encouraged me to follow my instincts and promised to return in six months to see how I was doing. My life couldn't be happier. Sometimes, I had to pinch myself to make sure I wasn't dreaming.

The Epilogue

Life continued at the stables, busy as usual but there was sadness around Hattie. She seemed quite lost without Fado. Justin tried all sorts of things to cheer her up. Her girls' came to stay at the farm, and her son invited her up to stay with him.

Things changed about six months later when she was on Skype to Fado.

"Hey, Hattie, now that I have found my family and resettled them, it's time you came out to meet everyone."

"Oh, Fado, I would love to, but I don't know how I can leave the stables for a couple of weeks."

"Yes, you can. Sheila will manage fine without you. Please, Hattie. It's very important to me. I've told them all about you."

"OK, give me a few weeks and I'll see what I can do."

Justin thought it was just what Hattie needed and began looking for flights on the internet. Sheila was relieved that some of the sparkle had returned to Hattie's eyes as she prepared for the trip.

Three weeks later she was on the plane. Loving Kenya when she had visited it before, Hattie felt really excited about the trip.

Fado was waiting for her at Nairobi airport. They hugged for a long time. With tears streaming they got into Fado's jeep. Fado talked non-stop. He was thrilled to have found his family. Their lives had been transformed thanks to Fado.

Hattie thought his mother to be a beautiful lady. She was gentle and kind but also strong and very talented. She had made amazing tapestries which not only decorated every house in the village, but were bought by people in high society. She also sold her handmade clothes to some of the best shops in the city. Fado was very proud of her. His eldest brother had set up as a carpenter. His brother helped him in their workshop when he wasn't at college. His sister was studying and had begun to write Fado's story. She already had articles published in Kenyan newspapers and magazines.

Hattie was overwhelmed at the family's drive and achievements in such a short time since Fado had rescued them from being servants. They welcomed her with open arms into the heart of the family and she felt really happy with them. Hattie loved the wildlife and being at one with nature.

It was exciting going off with Fado to look for horses. Buying a thoroughbred mare gave Fado the opportunity to breed himself. Hattie encouraged Fado's ideas to continue with his passion for horses. He was a very talented horseman.

All too soon, her holiday was over but she had gained a new family who she would never forget.